The Silver Swan

THE SILVER SWAN

Elena Delbanco

OTHER PRESS

Production Editor: Yvonne E. Cárdenas
Text Designer: Julie Fry
This book was set in Perpetua, Priory, and Bellevue by
Alpha Design & Composition of Pittsfield, NH.

10 9 8 7 6 5 4 3 2 1

Printed in the United States of America on acid-free paper. For information write to Other Press LLC, 2 Park Avenue, 24th Floor, New York, NY 10016.
Or visit our Web site: www.otherpress.com

Library of Congress Cataloging-in-Publication Data

Delbanco, Elena.
The silver swan : a novel / by Elena Delbanco.
pages cm
ISBN 978-1-59051-716-1 (alk. paper) — ISBN 978-1-59051-717-8 (ebook)
1. Cellists—Fiction. 2. Musicians—Fiction. 3. Fathers and daughters—Fiction. 4. Family secrets—Fiction. I. Title.
PS3604.E4245S55 2015
813'.6—dc23

2014017041

Publisher's Note:
This is a work of fiction. Names, characters, places, and incidents either are the product of the author's imagination or are used fictitiously, and any resemblance to actual persons, living or dead, events, or locales is entirely coincidental.

For Nicholas, forever

The silver swan, who living had no note,
As death approached, unlocked her silent throat.
Leaning her breast against the reedy shore,
Thus sang her first and last, and sang no more.
"Farewell all joy, oh death come close mine eyes,
More geese than swans now live, more fools than wise."

—Orlando Gibbons, "The Swan Song," Old English madrigal, 1612

PROLOGUE

1980

Because the wood floor creaks in the long corridor, Mariana can hear her father approaching. She turns toward the door. As it opens, she looks down at the small cello she has been playing and tightly grips the bow. Alexander Feldmann leans against the doorframe. He wears a silk paisley dressing gown and embroidered slippers. With a cigarette in a tortoiseshell holder in his hand, he stares at her, exhaling smoke. "Mariana, you're flat. That A is too flat."

Sixty years old, Alexander is well over six feet, handsome, with dark hair now silvered at the temples; his brown eyes are deep set, his chin strong. Mixed in with the tobacco, Mariana smells his lavender eau de cologne. He chides her gently, less irritably. "You're not stretching far enough, sweetheart. When your hands have grown a little, this won't be so difficult."

Looking down at her cello, she nods.

"You're noodling around, Mariana, you're not really practicing. I can tell. And why are you sitting on your desk chair? Your feet can't reach the floor. How can you play when you're not stable or grounded?"

"I don't like to sit on the little chair, Papa. I put it in the closet. It's too small."

He laughs and comes to stand behind her. Mariana feels shy with her father, who is rarely home. World famous as a performer, he has a schedule of concerts that keeps him away; he is already booked for the next three years. And during his days in Manhattan, Alexander is preoccupied with his own daily hours of practice and giving cello lessons in his studio in the apartment. His students, from Juilliard, come and go all day, each for an appointed hour.

Now he touches her shoulder, amused. "Mama told me that you erased Eric Katz's name and put yours on my list for a lesson today. That was naughty."

"I know you're leaving again," she whispers. "First thing tomorrow morning."

"And?"

She pauses, looking away. "I wanted to be with you."

Alexander takes another puff of his cigarette. "Well, when you finish practicing, you may join us for breakfast. Your mother and I do need to talk before I go to Switzerland."

He leans down and takes her left hand, showing her the position she needs to reach the A properly. His face is smooth, the scent of his aftershave strong. Sweeping her hair aside, he gently kisses her neck. She closes her eyes. He whispers, "You must work harder, sweetheart. It takes more than talent to be a great cellist. It takes *hard* work, dedication." As he leaves her room, he says, "For a special treat, if you work hard on the Sarabande this morning, I'll let you play it for me on the Silver Swan, after breakfast. We'll eat when you're done."

Then he is gone. Mariana waits for a moment. She reaches her hand to her hair and smells it dreamily for traces of him.

When he is away, she sneaks into his room and puts drops of his scent on her fingers. Then she rushes back to her own room and rubs her fingers on her pillowcase. The fragrance soothes her, helps her sleep.

Again she starts to play. In her nightgown, Mariana is working on Bach. She is tall for an eight-year-old, all arms and legs and angles; the seeds of future beauty have been planted in her face. As she leans forward, her long, dark hair falls over the instrument. She brushes it away with her right arm, lifting the bow impatiently. Forcing herself to concentrate, she repeats the opening measures of the Sarabande from the G-Major Suite. Filtered through venetian blinds, sun rises over the rooftops of Fifth Avenue across the wintry park. Though her bedroom door is closed, in the pauses while she rests she can hear her parents' voices raised in disagreement.

When twenty minutes have passed—a clock hangs on the bedroom wall, exacting and reproachful—she places the bow on the music stand and hops off her chair. Then, having set her instrument carefully down on the rug, she walks the long, dark corridor past the dining room and kitchen to what her parents call "the dinette," where they await her. It is eight in the morning, a Sunday in mid-February. The walls of the apartment have just been painted—this is a choice of her mother's—charcoal gray.

❦

The dinette is small, with a round table and molded pedestal chairs. Her own chair tips when Mariana climbs onto it, sitting between her father and mother and keeping her eyes on the table, not looking at the wall, which has been recently papered. The pattern makes her dizzy: thin stripes of pale green and brown that, if she watches closely, waver. She shuts her eyes, then opens them, and the stripes merge and converge.

Her parents have stopped arguing. They are smoking and drinking espresso. A newspaper is folded at her mother's place, her eyeglasses, with their silver cord, resting on it. Her white hair is thick and unbrushed. Though Alexander urges her to color it, she will not. A great beauty once (so Mariana has been told and can see in the framed photographs of the young Pilar), her mother resolutely refuses to "keep herself up." That is her father's phrase when reproachful or angry, and he seems angry now. Pilar too is clad in a bathrobe. It is neither silk nor paisley, but nylon and black. When Alexander is away, she often wears it all day.

As Mariana reaches for the pitcher of orange juice, her mother says, not looking at her,

"Mariana, you know I don't like you to go barefoot. Where are your slippers?"

"I'm sorry."

"Let her be," says Alexander. "It's the day of rest..."

Her mother has tears in her eyes. Mariana knows her parents often fight before her father leaves on tour. This makes her both anxious and sad. Pilar places a plate of toast in front of her and pours a glass of juice, silent. "Thank you," Mariana says, and tries to touch her mother's hand, but she has pulled it away. The girl swallows what she barely chews. Dutifully, she slips down off her pedestal chair to retrieve her slippers. As she leaves the dinette, her father folds his napkin, takes one last sip of coffee, and tells her to join him in the studio.

"You've done a nice job this morning," he says. "Now come and play the Sarabande for me on the Silver Swan."

In her slippers, she runs the length of the apartment to Alexander's studio. As is the case with her bedroom, it looks out over Central Park. Here, however, the windows are unobstructed and sunlight floods the room. A concert grand Steinway, covered in a woven shawl of orange and gold, stands against one wall. The opposite wall has shelves from floor to ceiling, filled with music manuscripts and recordings and file boxes of Alexander's reviews. Also on the shelves are many photographs of him in evening clothes, onstage or backstage or with other musicians, shaking hands and smiling. There are citations and framed album covers and a Grammy Award and two Grand Prix du Disque.

A pair of cello cases stand in a corner, both closed. In the room's center, on a worn Persian rug, two chairs face each other. A small table holds a metronome and an ashtray filled with cigarette butts. The great Catalan cellist Pablo Casals, her father tells her, smoked a pipe while playing. When they opened up the maestro's cello, Alexander says, there were match heads and tobacco and even an old coin that had fallen through one of the f-holes and rattled around inside.

She giggles. "But we'll be much more careful," says her father, "won't we, with the Silver Swan?" He tells Mariana to sit in the chair facing his, then goes to one of the cases and carefully removes what he calls his treasure, the great love of his life. "I am speaking only of music, of course," he says. "*You* are the love of my life when I'm speaking of people."

"And Mama?" she asks. He doesn't answer.

As he brings the Stradivarius toward her, Alexander turns the instrument this way and that in the morning sun. The varnish glows a warm golden-orange. It absorbs yet engenders the light, sending flashes of sunlight across the walls.

"Beautiful, isn't it, sweetheart?" He holds the Swan up beside her. "Let's find our secret sign."

At the crest of the cello's dark scroll, Mariana studies two one-inch silver engravings: matched medallions of a swan poised for flight above the wooden pegs. The carvings, though small, are intricate. There is a story about them, one he has told her often. An artist called Benvenuto Cellini, a very famous Italian, used the pattern of a swan for a silver sculpture he made to decorate a container for salt. Somehow someone cut it up, and Stradivari was given the little swans to keep. When he built this instrument, he fitted the birds' metal profiles onto the carved wooden scroll. "That's why it's called the Silver Swan. This happened in 1712—can you believe it?—more than sixty years before America became America. And now this great cello, this work of art, belongs to me, to *us*."

On one side of the mirroring paired images, Alexander's own initials form part of the design, added to the filigree, an etched *AF* on the feathers of a wing. Her father has told Mariana that only three people in the world—he, she, and her mother—are aware of the existence of these additional marks. And the man who did the markings (here Alexander drops his voice) took his knowledge to the grave. So it is *our* family secret, *our* hidden sign, and the way you, Mariana Alexandra Feldmann, will always be able to recognize the authentic cello. There are lots of ugly ducklings, Alexander says, but only one true Swan. He tunes the instrument.

She watches her father's long strong fingers, as he turns the wooden pegs. When he has finished tuning, he puts the gleaming Swan between her knees and kneels beside her on the carpet. He strokes her cheek. She is transfixed.

"All right, my angel, play beautifully for your papa." He stands again. "One day, we'll rent Carnegie Hall and we'll choose the same date as my debut there in 1945. That happens to have been your birthday," he reminds her. "Twenty-seven years later, you arrived on that exact date. It's our magic number." Mariana wonders if she would like to work so hard on her birthday but does not interrupt. She knows this story well, too. "A day I could never forget," he says. "My debut. This is how I remember your birthday."

"You'll be away again this year," she murmurs, but Alexander is lost in his fantasy.

"We'll go to Bergdorf Goodman to buy you a glamorous dress and you'll choose the color. I'll be very proud of you, won't I?" He holds her chin gently, his face close to hers. She doesn't answer.

"Remember, best of all," he repeats. "On that day, you'll play the Swan."

CHAPTER ONE

Mariana

2010

The winter had been hard and long: snow, rain, a sudden thaw, then snow again. By mid-April, finally, the ground had cleared. Mariana was on her way to Boston to meet her father's lawyer. As the plane landed at Logan, she pulled on her knee-high leather boots, fastened her hair with a tortoise clip, and returned her book to the Hermès bag between her feet. She was coming from New York for the day and carried no luggage. The man across the aisle, with whom she'd briefly spoken as they boarded, watched her unabashedly. At almost six feet, a dark and angular beauty, she was used to such attention; men had been staring at her for years. Crossing her legs and pressing them against the tray in front of her, she leaned back in her own cramped seat. Wind gusts, the pilot warned them, might be strong. Turbulence did not bother her.

Once at the gate, she unbuckled her belt and reached into the overhead bin for the rain cape it seemed she was going to need. Draping it around her shoulders, Mariana hoisted her bag and waited to deplane. Now her high-heeled boots felt tight, and she regretted having removed them for the flight.

Her father had died suddenly in his house in the Berkshires on January 10, ten days after his ninetieth birthday party. Because he and Mariana were just about to share their ritual cocktail at five thirty, she was able to give the coroner an almost exact accounting of the timing of his fall: five twenty-eight. Waiting impatiently, on the second-floor landing, shouting for his nurse-attendant, he had raised himself from his wheelchair, become entangled in his oxygen tubing, and clattered down the long flight of stairs. Mariana, in the kitchen, ran to him, but he was unconscious. The nurse dialed 911. Mariana blamed herself. Had she been standing near her father—not staring out the kitchen window at the snowdrifts and the blowing snow—she might have caught him as he tumbled from the wheelchair, or might have broken his fall. She blamed the nurse as well.

Feldmann had survived his wife—who was fifteen years younger—by seven years. When her mother passed away on a clear, March morning, Mariana had been at her side. She and the hospice nurse had just finished changing their charge's nightgown and brushing back her silver hair. Pilar lay silent as the nurse gathered up the soiled clothes and sheets and took them to the laundry. Mariana held her mother's hand and studied her face, its sweet, peaceful expression. She spoke to her mother with the tenderness Pilar had so long rejected. These moments would have to satisfy her. They were what she would retain: a faint pressure on her hand, a sigh. She leaned down to whisper, "I love you, Mama." Mariana felt no breath. She cried out for the nurse.

At the moment his wife died, Alexander was in Poland, judging a competition. He hurried back, bemoaning his loss, proclaiming devotion to Pilar's memory and telling his consolers he could not go on without her. Feldmann performed his sadness, an oratorio of grief.

In late May 2003, he sold the apartment on Central Park West and moved to Stockbridge, in the Berkshires. He told Mariana he was tired of the city and ready to live "in nature." The family had long owned a summer place near Tanglewood that Alexander named "Swann's Way" although he'd never read a word of Proust. Mariana had packed up Alexander's apartment, closed up her own—a brownstone walk-up a few blocks away—and moved to Stockbridge with her father to care for him through the summer. The chamber music group she had played with since giving up her solo career, the New York Chamber Ensemble, did not perform in the summer months. When autumn came, she took a leave of absence to stay with Alexander. He said he could not survive without her, although he criticized her daily for forsaking her career.

Alexander required constant attention, and toward the end, Mariana was the only one left to provide it. She rarely left his side. One evening, shortly before his death, they sat together.

"Have I finished my martini, sweetheart?" Alexander's fingers, trembling on the surface of the marble table, felt for the stem of the glass he could not see.

"There's one more sip, Papa, and the olive's at the bottom," Mariana answered, edging the glass toward his hand. "And because it's almost Christmas, we'll celebrate. I'll make you another. A small one, a mini. But you mustn't get too sleepy before dinner. We have a lovely one tonight."

He lifted his glass to capture the last drops. "You take such good care of me, darling. You must be very dull in the country with only an old man and his old friends for company."

Mariana smiled at him. He had always confused the words "dull" and "bored," as did his parents, who were Viennese and spoke tentative English all their lives. She took pleasure in this residue of foreign speech and did not correct him. "I am not at all dull here. I have a great deal to do taking care of you. I've come to love our life in Stockbridge, and, besides, I can always return to New York for a few days if I get restless."

The old man was anxious. "You're not planning to go again soon, are you? I get very lonely when you leave me here with nurses who never have anything interesting to say and can't make a decent martini!" She laughed and stood up, reaching across the table to remove his glass. A small fire glowed across the room in the immense fireplace.

"No, I'm not leaving you. I haven't found one good reason to go to New York in months, except to check on my apartment. I'm staying here, Papa."

Outside, it was dark, and the holiday lights Mariana had strung on the evergreens in front of the house illumined the fresh snow. They had had no such lights when she was a child and they came to this house in the Berkshires for the holiday season. Her parents opposed them. "We are Jewish, after all," her mother said. But now her mother was dead, and her father took pleasure in the sparkling display. A large Christmas tree, cut on the property, stood in the entrance hall. Under it, Mariana had placed the presents for Alexander that arrived each day from friends and students and fans. There were many. He was impatient for Christmas morning and asked her often to tell him how many days he would have to wait.

"I'm going to the kitchen to fix your drink and tend to dinner," she announced, leaning down to kiss the top of his head.

"Why don't you play for a little while? This would be a good time." She positioned his wheelchair, turning it away from the table, and put on the brakes. The Silver Swan rested on the paisley shawl covering the grand piano. Mariana brought it to him. Then she applied resin to his bow. With the fire at his back, he began to play as she took up his empty glass and left the room.

Standing at the bar in the butler's pantry, Mariana opened the glass cabinet doors and removed the gin and vermouth. She filled the silver shaker with ice and carefully measured Alexander's martini, then poured herself a glass of white wine. Since her mother's death, they had spent so many evenings this way, alone or with company, winter and summer. Mariana had managed the beautiful old house, giving dinners and parties for the musicians who played at Tanglewood, inviting Alexander's friends, students, and former colleagues, and a few of her own, to visit. She had flown with him to dozens of "farewell" concerts, to master classes and competitions and festivals in Puerto Rico, Germany, Spain, France, Korea, China, Japan, and Argentina. But in the past year, he had grown frail, tired, and forgetful. His eyesight had failed. He wanted less company but kept her at his side.

The great irony for Mariana was that this life she now shared with Alexander was all her mother ever wanted. More and more despondent, her mother had waited for him to grow tired of traveling and concertizing, to come home, to take up a life with her—a life like this, shared evenings by the fire, idle conversation, hands touching as they watched the stars above the mountains. She felt deeply sad that her mother had missed Alexander's new sweetness, the gentle humor and tenderness he expressed in these last years. Gone were the fearsome outbursts of temper, the anger and egotism that terrorized her and suffocated Pilar. Here was this loving old man who needed her. Her mother had died too soon.

Alexander's night nurse was eating her dinner at the kitchen table. She smiled at Mariana, arching her eyebrow at the extra martini on the tray, but said nothing. The old man must have his small pleasures, they had all agreed. Returning to the living room, Mariana set the drinks on the table and sat down. Alexander was playing the G-Major Bach Suite, the one he best remembered. His eyes were closed. The Silver Swan, its sound a resonant liquid gold, filled the room and vibrated in her chest. As she listened and sipped her wine, she imagined the Swan in the eighteenth-century Cremonese atelier where it was created; she saw another old man, brush in hand, applying his expert strokes of varnish as the instrument itself became a glistening source of light. This treasure, passed down through centuries and now possessed by Alexander Feldmann, would soon enough be hers.

The best violoncelli had names. She remembered some of them: the Bass of Spain, the Gore-Booth, and the Piatti. They were often named after the people who owned or performed on them: the Batta, the Countess of Stanlein, the Paganini, the Servais, the Duport, the Davidoff. "Perhaps," Alexander often said, "this will become the Feldmann. It may someday be named for me."

❦

He came to the end of the suite and, exhausted, let his bow arm fall to his side. Mariana took the instrument from him. On the piano she saw the soft cloth he used to wipe the residue of resin off the varnish. She retrieved it and, by the light of the lamp, cleaned the wood under the bridge.

"Don't put it away just yet, darling," Alexander murmured. "I would like to hear you play the Swan for me with the strength of your youth. I find I no longer can make it sing."

"I can't say I agree," she answered. "You've lost very little." This was not exactly true, but it was what her father wanted to hear. With her free hand, she moved a chair in front of him and placed the Swan between her legs. "What do you want me to play?"

"The D Major," he said. She paused a moment and then plunged into the suite with force. He sat—eyes closed, smiling—and with his right hand beat time.

Mariana returned the Swan to the safe in Alexander's studio and wheeled him to the dining room for dinner, drawing his chair up to the head of the long, polished table. She lit candles on the sideboard, tucked his napkin under his chin, and went to the kitchen. Returning with two bowls of onion soup, she joined him.

"I wonder how I shall be remembered," Alexander began. Mariana sighed, anticipating another dinner spent discussing her father's legacy, but she humored him as usual. "Really, Papa, your recordings will be played forever. No one will surpass your performance of the Dvořák concerto."

"How sad," he continued, "that I never recorded the Bach suites. I waited too long, it appears. That is a great loss for the world." Feldmann paused. "I wonder if it's too late." Mariana didn't answer. She too wished he had recorded them, but it was certainly too late. As they finished dinner, he grew troubled. "My sweetheart," he said, patting Mariana's hand, "you are so good to me. But what will you do when I'm gone?" He paused again. "You know I have been ready to die for a long time now, but I cannot—because I know how much you need me and depend on me."

Mariana suppressed exasperation as he looked at her wistfully.

"You should have a husband."

"I had many a boyfriend as a kid, Papa, and you made it very difficult for all of them…and for me. Remember how intimidating you could be? She smiled as she said this, but clearly she was annoyed. "I think you were jealous every time I went out. You scared everyone away. And when I fell in love with Pietovsky, I thought you'd have a stroke, you were so agitated," she continued, an edge in her voice.

"Well, he was a married man, Mariana, and no good for you. What father would want that for his daughter? All we wanted, your mother and I, was that you find a good husband."

She stared at him in disbelief. "If I had a husband, good or bad, I couldn't have lived here with you for all these years."

"And," he continued, ignoring her answer, "you should never have stopped playing; you had such a rare talent. Such a tragedy. I hold Pietovsky responsible for this."

"And yet you remained dear friends."

"You should have had a fantastic career. Your life was unfolding so brilliantly."

"Don't blame Pietovsky. Besides, if I had had a great career, I would have been playing a concert somewhere in Europe tonight. Mama would have died alone, and you would be here with only your nurses for company."

Again, he ignored her. "And certainly, if you weren't going to have a great career, you should have had a child. You are so nurturing, darling."

"Oh, Papa." She sighed again, getting up to clear away the dishes. "I have had a child, believe me. I still have a child. He is about to turn ninety years old, and yet he's still a child." She leaned down to kiss his cheek and went for the night nurse.

❧

The Prudential Building loomed in the distance. From the taxi, Mariana could see joggers on the towpath by the Charles River, and bicyclists, and people walking dogs. She was about to meet Christopher Beecher of Beecher, Hamilton, Stein & Snow; Alexander had retained him when he established legal residence in the state of Massachusetts. The meeting today would clarify what she could expect from the Feldmann estate. As its sole heir, she would be rich. In addition to the Silver Swan, now estimated to be worth at least ten million dollars, and possibly a good deal more, there were nine copies of the great original—nowhere near as valuable, of course, but fine to play and worth a collective half million at least. There were bows and cash and stock market investments and the Berkshire property. Lawyers and accountants often warned Feldmann about taxes, and estate planners offered their advice. Had her father transferred ownership of the Swan to her years earlier, or sold it, or established a trust, the government would not now be poised to take such a large share of her inheritance. Yet he retained possession of the instrument, claiming he would own it until his death, an event he simply could not foresee. He would say, "*If I die*," not "*When*..."

At the lawyer's office, Mariana was greeted by an elderly receptionist and then by Christopher Beecher himself, a short gentleman with a shock of white hair, piercing blue eyes, and a slightly hunched back that made him appear somehow kindly. His shirt was blue, his tie striped red and green. Horn-rimmed glasses on a black elastic ribbon dangled at his chin. Beecher invited her into his book-paneled office, where he explained that Alexander had particularly requested this meeting for a reading of the will, though such a face-to-face encounter was no longer necessary. "It is, I'm afraid, more a function of television shows and films than legal practice nowadays, but it was your father's wish and we chose to honor it."

"I'm glad you did. It's a pleasure to meet you..."

"Yes." His voice was high. "A personal association is always preferable, is it not, to fax machines and xeroxed documents arriving in the mail? And I do want to tell you how much I admired your father; I have a whole *shelf* of recordings, and I went to his concerts whenever he played in Boston. You know, I came to the memorial service in New York, though I did not introduce myself to you at the time. You were so occupied."

She nodded. The memorial service had taken place on March 25, at the 92nd Street Y. Hundreds of people attended. Alexander's students spoke. Few of his peers were still alive, and the men and women onstage were no longer young. Thirty-, forty-, fifty-, and even sixty-year-olds saluted their lost master, describing how he'd taught them, how he'd changed their bow arm or vibrato or understanding of the instrument, how generous he'd been and how important, crucial even, to the course of their careers. Most passionately, they talked of the deep understanding of music he offered them. At the ceremony's end, sixteen cellists came onstage to play the Casals "Song of the Birds" in his honor. Many wept.

"In any case," Beecher continued, "your father wanted you to read a letter he entrusted to me just before he passed."

"Oh?"

Beecher handed her a sealed envelope: cream colored, thick, with her name in a familiar scrawl in black ink on the front. "This is for you."

Mariana was surprised. She asked the lawyer if he knew the letter's contents or had, in fact, read it himself.

"It's signed across the back, you see. And no, I have not read it. It is — that old-fashioned concept — confidential."

She wondered what the letter could contain. The two of them had lived together, after all, and she had overseen his mail, paid his bills. This letter would no doubt offer some instructions for a scholarship program he planned to establish or what she should do with the Stradivarius copies or do to the roof at Swann's Way.

The lawyer withdrew from the room; she opened the letter and read:

December 10, 2009

My dear Mariana,

I think perhaps this is the first letter I've written to you since you were a small child and I was traveling in France. And to think it will come to you when I am gone is very strange. But there are things you must know in order to understand how I have organized my legacy — things I meant to tell you when your mother died. Because you were distressed at that time and had already decided to give up your solo career, I never found occasion to reveal these things to you. After a while, I simply decided not to.

As I'm sure you have known and been much affected by, your mother and I were not happy together. I shall spare you the details but tell you that she resented my absence as my concert schedule increased; she resented my success, my students — she even resented you — anything that took my attention away from her. It was an unnatural dependence, and as she grew more withdrawn, refusing to travel with me or share in the pleasures of my fame, I developed a close relationship with another woman, someone you have met only once before, the Swiss singer Francine Roselle.

Mme Roselle and I were both married to others throughout the years of our affair, she to the conductor Bernard Roselle. We saw each other only when we could, but our love was intense and passionate. As you may perhaps remember, Francine had something to do with my acquisition of the Silver Swan, long ago in Strasbourg. It was her mother who introduced me to the owner of the instrument. Over the years I taught Francine's son, Claude — he is three years your junior, and I have been very proud of his career: he is a fine cellist. His father is an excellent conductor, if somewhat uninspired. In some ways — since you, alas, no longer perform as a soloist — Claude has come to be my musical heir. I hope you will be friends. Your mother, I believe, never knew of my relationship with Mme Roselle, for we were together only in Europe.

This information changes nothing in your life, dear Mariana. You are my beloved, my only daughter, and I have always protected you, as I shall continue to through the disposition of my estate. But your knowledge of this will help you accept what is to come. I have written this letter, sealed it, and given it to my lawyer, Christopher Beecher, whom you will now have met. No one else is apprised of this information—besides you and, of course, Mme Roselle, though she does not know I have told you of our relationship. You have been a devoted daughter. I have never understood what caused you to stop playing. But now, at least, I can offer you the fruits of my long life in art.

Be free, my angel, to live your own life at last.

Papa

Alone in the office, Mariana pressed her hands to her face. How could it be possible that neither she nor her mother had suspected this long, treacherous affair? How could he think this changed nothing? Had her mother actually known about Francine Roselle? How terrible if she *had* known, or suspected it. This would explain the tears, the dark silence in the house whenever Alexander got ready to leave. Every time he went on tour, he went to open arms abroad. Pilar must have felt the pain of his eagerness to go.

Mariana put the letter in her purse and rose from her chair. She wiped away her tears with the back of her trembling hand. The lawyer knocked. Courteously, he opened the door and beckoned her to follow. Mariana walked behind him to the conference room where, she assumed, he would read Feldmann's will to her. As he opened the oak door to usher her in, Beecher turned to face her. "Your father left very strict instructions for this occasion. I hope things will turn out to everyone's satisfaction."

"Everyone?"

But Beecher had entered the conference room.

⁂

The table gleamed. Large windows framed the street, the rise of Beacon Hill beyond, the shops and cars below. There were green-shaded lamps, dark leather chairs, a water pitcher and four glasses on a tray. Two people—a young man and a much older woman—were seated at the table. "You've met before," said Christopher Beecher. "But unless I'm much mistaken, it's been a very long time."

The elegant man stood to greet her. From the photos on her father's wall, she understood that this was Claude Roselle—but he was even more handsome in person. In most of those pictures, Claude wore a tuxedo; today he was attired in a slim, dark gray Italian suit. He approached, his hand outthrust, smile flashing. He held her hand with both his own and pumped it warmly, eagerly, looking into her eyes.

"How wonderful to meet you, Mariana."

She stared at him, then at the woman sitting at the far end of the table. This must be Alexander's lover, Francine Roselle, the woman who'd drawn him away from Pilar and from Mariana as well. No photograph of Claude's mother adorned her father's studio wall, but here, clearly, was the singer who'd been Feldmann's mistress, and for whom his love had been—as she'd just read—"intense and passionate."

Christopher Beecher was saying, "And do you remember, or may I present, Mme Francine Roselle?"

The woman stood. She was short, plump, and still lovely, her skin unlined. Her hair, dyed a pale silvery blond, was carefully coiffed, and she wore a slate-blue traveling suit and embroidered white silk blouse. Strands of pearls enclosed her neck. Mariana would not have known her on the street, but seeing Francine now revived in her the mysterious feeling of unease she'd felt whenever Alexander mentioned—in passing, as he'd often done—her name. Claude had retained her hand. "I so loved and admired your father. He was the most inspired of artists and teachers. I'm deeply grateful to have been his student."

Francine Roselle pushed back her chair and came around the table, reaching up to kiss Mariana on both cheeks. Mariana froze. The smell of the woman's skin was familiar: L'Heure Bleue—the Guerlain perfume her father always brought her from Europe, and which she'd never liked. Pilar had told him that the perfume was unsuitable for a young girl, but Alexander continued to purchase it, no doubt in haste, at the airport duty-free shop on his way home. Or perhaps he'd taken it from Francine's supply. All his gifts were tokens, Pilar complained, all his kindnesses perfunctory or rushed. Francine drew back, removing her hands from Mariana's arms as if she'd touched something terribly hot.

"We haven't met for such a long time, my dear. I wanted to write to you the very *moment* of your father's death. I would have come to his memorial service, but I had a concert engagement and was unable to cancel." She clasped her hands as her eyes teared up. "His death deeply affected us. We will greatly miss him."

"Yes," said Claude. "It has been so difficult. Maman cried for weeks. We were—*are*—all so devastated. What a loss."

"How are *you*, Mariana?" Francine asked.

"I'm sad of course." Mariana said coldly, moving around the table. She waited for the lawyer to indicate her place. He did so, and she sat. But *why*, she asked herself, beginning to tremble, were these two people also present? Mme Roselle must now be, although she did not look it, not less than seventy years old. Why had she been asked to come to Boston, and to Beecher's office?

She tried to imagine a reason. Perhaps these two intended to make an offer to buy the Stradivarius; perhaps her father had arranged it so they would have the chance to purchase the Swan, a right of first refusal. At her place there was a legal pad and a pen.

"What a loss," Claude said again. "You must feel it keenly. You two were so close, I'm told." Mariana turned and, studying him, found him disturbingly attractive. She could not look away, despite his mother's attempt to engage her.

"How do you occupy yourself now?" Francine asked.

"I've had a lot to attend to," she answered, "as you can imagine. He never paid attention to his affairs." Saying this, she paused, embarrassed. "I mean, his financial affairs, of course."

Beecher proposed they proceed with the meeting. Claude pulled out a chair and sat next to her, resting his arm across the back of her chair, while Francine returned to her seat at the far end of the table. Mariana thanked Claude for the glass of water he had poured and looked quickly away. She was drawn to him, to the strong angles of his face, his mixture of mature self-confidence, sincerity, and boyish charm. He had dark blue eyes and thick curls, fair like his mother's. She knew very little about him, though she had read reviews, of course, which Alexander pressed on her. He was a rising star in Europe, much engaged and respected, and in the letter her father had called him "my musical heir."

"Your attention, please," said the lawyer, "we may as well begin." Beecher thanked them each in turn for coming. He had scheduled this session, as Claude Roselle knew, to coincide with the musician's debut concert in New York, so that it would not be necessary to travel twice to America.

He wished the young cellist luck. Looking at Mariana, he smiled. "I must iterate that it was your father's explicit wish we be together in this room."

Beecher droned on, "There are the usual assertions—'being of sound mind and body'—the usual disclaimers—'revoking all previous such documents, etc.'" Mariana tried to ignore the stirring proximity of young Roselle at her side, his arm across the back of her chair, almost embracing her. She turned quickly to glance at him and found that he was staring back, his eyes deep pools of concern and sympathy. Beecher continued talking, ". . . and the usual small bequests to housekeepers and relatives—your father's nephew, I believe, now resident in Israel—and to the Cello Society and the Koussevitzky Memorial Fund at Tanglewood. And so on and so forth. I will of course be glad to discuss each of these in detail, but none of them need properly concern us now. Instead, and again as per Alexander Feldmann's instructions, I am to inform you in person of the principal bequests herein. Any questions?"

They shook their heads. Mariana tried not to look at Claude. Her hands shook.

Settling his glasses on his nose, the lawyer read:

(1) To my daughter Mariana Feldmann I leave the property in Stockbridge and all my stocks, savings, pensions, and personal effects.

(2) To Mariana I leave my collection of the nine copies of the Silver Swan, which I purchased or commissioned from stringed instrument makers, and my collection of bows, to be disposed of at her discretion.

(3) To Mariana I leave all my papers and music manuscripts.

(4) To Claude Roselle, in recognition of his great artistry and his special relationship to me as my gifted student, and because my daughter no longer performs as a soloist, I leave the Stradivarius violoncello of 1712, known as the Silver Swan.

Mariana pushed back her chair and stood up abruptly. "No, that can't be true. Read it again," she cried out. As Beecher reread the final bequest, she began to weep. Alexander had betrayed her. Claude reached for her arm, but she flung him away. Grabbing her bag and coat, she ran out of the room, down the book-lined corridor, and out the door.

CHAPTER TWO

Claude

After the meeting in Boston, Claude and his mother went their separate ways. While she paid a visit to friends in Cambridge, he flew directly to New York to prepare for his American debut. On his way to the airport, Claude thought about Mariana and her evident distress. It disturbed him to have stayed in Beecher's office while she fled in tears. He had wanted to go after her, to catch and comfort her. He imagined holding her and gently dabbing the tears off her beautiful face with his handkerchief, stroking her astonishing hair. But why did he want to? He had always been distressed by turbulent emotions, especially in women and especially if he felt that he might in any way have caused them. Casual relationships, those that came without demands or requests for commitment, suited him best. And yet women always seemed to want more than he intended to give, if not at first, then eventually.

Arriving in New York, Claude checked into the Regency Hotel on Park Avenue, his mother's choice. He tried several times to call his girlfriend, Sophie von Auer, in Lugano, wanting to tell her about the Stradivarius and his great good luck, but Sophie was away on a two-day retreat with personnel from the museum where she worked and could not be reached. He left only guarded messages on her mobile, not wanting to spoil the surprise. Then he ate a light room-service supper and fell into jet-lagged sleep.

When he awoke, he called the offices of Baum & Fernand. Christopher Beecher had told him the Stradivarius was in New York, consigned by Alexander just before his death, for safekeeping and restoration, to the shop of the instrument dealer, Heinrich Baum, and his partner, the luthier Pierre Fernand. Claude was told by the receptionist that neither man would be available that day. Both were traveling, she said, but would return tomorrow, and then he could certainly have an appointment. He informed her that his errand concerned the Stradivarius, and she said Mr. Beecher had indeed called. Mr. Baum was aware of the reason for his visit and had left instructions to make Mr. Roselle welcome the next morning at eleven, if that would be suitable. Claude said, "Tomorrow at eleven, by all means."

Therefore he had a day to practice, and did so in his hotel room, using a mute and playing his David Tecchler, the cello he'd bought for himself ten years earlier. He worked on the Brahms sonatas that he was to play at Alice Tully Hall, going over the difficult passages, experimenting with new phrasing and fingerings, but always returning to those Feldmann had taught him. Next he worked for a while on the Schumann concerto he would play on his national tour. When his hands grew tired, he went out for lunch and then walked until he found his way to Lincoln Center. There, outside Alice Tully Hall, he saw a poster with his name and photograph: Claude Roselle and—without a picture—William Rossen. "The acclaimed Swiss violoncellist," Claude read, "is making his New York debut on Saturday, April 10, at 8 p.m. This will be the first appearance of his American tour." For the publicity photo, his hair had been carefully gelled and tousled, and his eyes were wide. He looked, he thought with amusement, very Euro.

As he walked, he continued thinking about Mariana and wondered if she lived alone or if he were anywhere near her neighborhood. In a city the size of New York, he would have to make a concerted effort to find her, unless he asked someone directly. "Concerted," he thought, and smiled—he was making a pun in English. He must find her and invite her to his debut. They had so much in common, so much to share, he believed—above all, their devotion to her father.

That night he went to dinner with his manager's American affiliate and the pianist William Rossen. He and Rossen planned to start rehearsals the next day. The dinner was a pleasant one. Over Thai food they talked about financial regulation and how it might affect Swiss banks, the death of Alexander, the volcano erupting in Iceland, and the health of the conductor James Levine. Claude wished he could turn the conversation to the subject of Mariana to find out more about her, but he could not find a subtle way to do so. When he returned to the hotel, a message awaited him. His mother had arrived and would see him for breakfast at nine.

❧

The next morning, at the hotel restaurant, the maître d' escorted them to a cloth-covered table near a window.

"Well"—Francine settled back in her chair—"we have had a great surprise, *mon petit*, you've received a remarkable gift. And an unexpected one. I had no idea my old friend would be so generous to you."

Claude, hair still wet from the shower, played with the teaspoon in his cup. "Maman, did you really not know of this in advance? I assumed, somehow, you did."

"No, darling, really not, though of course I always wished you would have such a great instrument, and I did wonder what Alexander would do with the Swan after Mariana stopped playing."

"She hasn't exactly stopped playing, Maman," Claude said. "She's been taking care of her father." He paused. "Perhaps she intends to resume her career. That's possible."

Francine ignored him. "I did wonder why we had been summoned to Boston by the lawyer, and I began to suspect there was a surprise in store. You know, of course, he was tremendously proud of you. Alexander always said you were his finest student."

"After Mariana," Claude corrected her. "He spoke *most* highly of her."

"That's true. But when she stopped playing, you became his great hope. Now, my darling, *you* are indeed the heir to his sound, his musical ideas, his virtuosity, and . . . his Stradivarius."

"I can't pretend I'm not thrilled. I feel immensely fortunate. I could hardly sleep last night thinking about seeing the Swan today. But the way Mariana ran away made me feel guilty—as if we'd stolen it from her." He looked at his mother and smiled. "Of course, I would not like to give it back."

"You will not be asked to. She knows this is what her father wanted."

"Maman, do you know why she gave up concertizing as a soloist? Perhaps—you were such intimate friends—M. Feldmann told you." Claude paused. "It does seem strange to stop playing so abruptly in the midst of such a big career."

"Alexander never explained it to me. I think, perhaps, he didn't even know the actual reason himself. But he always said it had something to do with her mother's illness and death—that she was profoundly depressed." Francine spread marmalade on her brioche and took a bite. "And," she continued, a look of dark disapproval on her face, "it might have had something to do with the extremely shocking and ridiculously public affair she carried on for several years with the Russian conductor Anton Pietovsky—a married man, almost her father's age. Everyone knew about it. Everyone talked about it. They traveled together and didn't even try to hide their relationship. But then Pietovsky threw her over and went back to his wife."

"What happened to Mariana?" Claude asked, fascinated.

"She was rumored to have suffered terribly from a broken heart."

"And stopped playing?"

"Oh, who knows, darling. It's none of our concern." She paused to chew. "Don't you remember how often Alexander would hint that one day the cello might be yours? Apparently, he wasn't just teasing you."

"But I never thought he meant it. Did you?" He studied his mother's face.

"It would have come to his daughter, I'm certain, if she'd continued her career, but she chose to stop. What use would she have for the instrument now? To play it in small, insignificant chamber music groups? Alexander wanted the Silver Swan in the hands of a great cellist with a great career. That's why it is now yours."

"It has a certain value, as you well know, and she might be in need of money."

"Well," Francine sniffed, "it's not as if he left her nothing. She has all his property and accounts, and she has those copies to sell if she chooses." She paused and declared, "Really, Claude, this is not our business."

"Nonetheless," he persisted, "I *am* concerned and I think I'll try to contact her. Maybe I'll invite her to my concert. I'd like very much to know her better." He pierced the egg yolk and watched it spread. "I found her very attractive, beautiful, in fact. Didn't you?"

Francine looked at him sharply but said nothing. Claude took a bite of his egg and picked up the *New York Times* Arts section. His mother turned her attention to her cell phone, arranging her schedule for the day. Claude sensed that his mother was annoyed with him and he did not want to upset her. Recently, when he'd called or visited, he found her crying, her face puffy and red, her neck wet with escaped tears. He did not want to ask her why she wept. He thought he might not like to know. During these times, his father was always away. Perhaps his absence was the reason for her distress, Claude had first surmised—some quarrel between them. As time went on, however, he thought not.

"I called Baum & Fernand yesterday and asked if I might come over and take a look at the Silver Swan—pay a visit and play a few notes. I have an appointment this morning at eleven. I wonder if you'd be willing to come with me. Please do, Maman. I'd so much like you to be there the first time I take the instrument out of its case as its rightful owner." He gave her his most fetching smile. "You were, should we say, 'instrumental' in my good fortune."

This mollified Francine. They went back to their rooms to collect what they'd need for the day. Departing the hotel, he carried his Tecchler with his left arm and held his mother's arm with his right. The sunlight was brilliant, the city alive with warm signs of spring. On Fifty-seventh Street, they headed west toward Carnegie Hall. His mother walked daintily, in high heels, her short legs unable to keep up with Claude's quick strides. He slowed his pace when she complained but found it difficult to contain his eagerness to hold the Silver Swan.

❧

After the loud bustle of the street, the shop was a refuge. Hushed and elegant, it smelled of wood and glue and varnish, belonging more to an older world, perhaps Cremona—that center of violin making—than to present-day Manhattan. The heavy glass doors creaked as Claude opened them. At this hour in the morning, the public showrooms were still quiet. Only a few customers had arrived to look at instruments. Antique wooden cabinets with glass fronts lined the walls of the two formal rooms. Warmly lit inside, they contained violins, violas, and cellos, all hung in the same direction, revealing many shades of glowing, polished wood that also caught the subdued light of the antique chandeliers. The floors were covered with frayed but splendid Persian carpets, and each room had a long antique French farm table at its center.

The young woman he had spoken with the day before greeted them and went off to fetch her employer. Claude and Francine unbuttoned their coats, and he stood his cello case against the wall. Many-paned floor-to-ceiling windows gave out over Fifty-seventh Street, but the traffic below was inaudible.

Heinrich Baum, a short, bald powerhouse of a man, came to greet them and shook their hands energetically. In his early seventies, he wore a dark blue suit with white stripes and a shirt sporting cuff links in the shape of violins. "Ah, Mme Roselle. You I have met when you came with Maestro Feldmann, but your son has not yet visited our shop. I am happy to welcome you here, M. Roselle, and to congratulate you on your great good fortune. It's a magnificent instrument, as you will see."

"He has seen it before, of course," said Francine. "We both know the cello."

"Yes, certainly," said Baum. "You were Alexander's friend."

Claude added, "I played the Swan several times during lessons, thanks to M. Feldmann's generosity. I know what a great treasure it is and, believe me, I know how very fortunate I am."

"Yes," Baum said ruefully, "it is indeed a treasure." He rubbed his hands and looked down. "As you no doubt are aware, I was involved in Feldmann's purchase of the Swan from the very beginning. I lent him the money to purchase it from the Gentner family, in Strasbourg. He paid me back promptly but, I will not pretend otherwise, I thought we had an understanding that our firm would sell the cello after Feldmann's death if Mariana were to decide to give it up. We are, of course, disappointed that this will not come to pass." He paused and managed a wry smile. "But our bad luck is your good fortune."

The three of them laughed uneasily. Francine said, "It was *my* good friend, Isabelle Gentner, who introduced Alexander to the family and made the sale possible. You see, we *all* have had a hand in this."

"And that's how my mother met M. Feldmann and how I, so fortunately, became his student."

"And how the cello has come into your possession," Baum said.

He then inquired if he might offer them coffee. Claude declined, saying his hands were already shaking with excitement and he'd best calm down if he were planning to play; Francine, however, accepted. The dealer was ceremonial. He spoke about the history of the Stradivarius. There was a trail to follow and he had followed it, he told the Roselles.

Claude listened intently as Baum spoke. In the future he would need to recite these histories. According to records, the Italian Count Crespi bought the Swan in 1714, and the family retained it for two or three generations. Then their republican sympathies forced them into exile. The cello found a new owner, a French military man who lived in Lorraine. Feldmann liked to tell the story he had heard from Mme Gentner—pointing to a faint discoloration on the back—of cognac spilled in argument.

The Swan was sold in Paris to J.-B. Vuillaume in 1854. From this point on the trail grew documented. Jean-Baptiste Vuillaume, as was well-known, championed Cremonese instruments. He was a first-rate copyist and patterned his own efforts on the model of the Swan. Using calipers to measure thickness, using the same width for blocks and ribs as did the long dead Italian, he followed the Swan template precisely. Its proportions and its f-holes and the placement of the sound post were all calculated to produce the largest and sweetest sound. No one could improve on it—or so Vuillaume had claimed. It was this Vuillaume that Mariana played.

Baum, having finished his lecture, excused himself to tell his partner, Pierre Fernand, that the Roselles had arrived. The receptionist led them to a small room and brought a silver tray with coffee and biscotti. Francine helped herself, even though she had just finished breakfast.

Baum returned with the luthier. Pierre Fernand wore a yellow smock with rolled-up sleeves over his clothes. He was a small man with pomaded hair combed back from his forehead and a gray mustache twirled at the ends. Behind him came Philippe Sorel, his assistant and manager of the workshop. He hung back and nodded a greeting. He too wore a smock.

Baum made introductions, and they all shook hands. "*Enchanté*," said Fernand, "*de vous revoir, Madame*, and to meet your son. I heard always that he is the artistic heir of M. Feldmann, but I see he is also so handsome." Francine responded that she too was pleased to see him again. "I am *désolé* about Alexandre," Fernand told the room. "You know, I always called him 'Maestro,' but he says to me, no, no, my name is Alexandre. We have lost a very great friend."

Although he had been living in America for decades, Fernand retained a strong French accent.

Even my mother's is milder, Claude thought, amused, and she has never lived in an English-speaking country.

"You know," continued the luthier, "this Swan is my *bébé*, my treasure. I am always the one who works on it, ever since M. Feldmann bring it back from Strasbourg. I myself was working for the great Maestro Sacconi, when I first came to this country and was, if you can believe it, young. I have waited many years for my chance to restore it, but M. Feldmann was always too busy playing. I hope you will understand, M. Roselle, that I promise him to attend to it."

"Of course," Claude said. "I would be honored to have you work on it. But can you tell me what kind of shape it's in right now? M. Feldmann himself got such a beautiful sound from the Swan, it never seemed to need improvement."

"Ah, this is not the problem. She sound very splendid, but she need care. She has a crack, tiny crack in the back and other things that must be repaired. The varnish needs cleaning, it gets a bit dull with the travels, changes in climate, dust. Some work on the sound post, an adjustment perhaps to the bridge — every great instrument deserves this, of course. I will make it sing even more beautifully. But you would like to see? Come, *M'sieurdame* to my workshop where is the safe."

With Baum and Sorel, Claude and Francine walked back, past the offices, toward the luthier's studio. It was large and light, the edges of the worktables lined with clamps. The walls held shelves with long planks of wood piled in stacks. White wooden blocks in boxes — their contents described by the date and place of acquisition — filled additional shelves. There were boxes labeled *Necks: Violin, Viola, Cello*, and a box labeled *Scrolls.*

A cabinet, its doors ajar, contained bottles of paint thinner and linseed oil and pigment and brushes and rags. Tools hung from large pieces of pegboard, and dismembered instruments rested on each workspace. Several, as yet unvarnished, were white. Wood shavings covered the floor; the smell of glue and varnish permeated the air. Four men were at work, wearing caps. They listened to music on a radio. Claude felt almost dizzy with excitement as Fernand unlocked the room-size safe and invited them to enter.

Within the safe, instruments hung from velvet straps, each in a separate stall. Inside these partitions sat wooden barrels filled to varying degrees with pieces of the instruments, if they had been disassembled: a neck, a scroll, a rib. One violin—a Guadagnini—had been taken completely apart; it rested in its barrel like a patient in intensive care after surgery. Here in the safe, the most valuable instruments were gathered, beneath little labels affixed to the stalls: Guarnerius, Amati, Stradivarius, Vuillaume. "As you see," Fernand said, "the Swan is not yet being operated on; she is intact."

"*Virga intacta*," joked Baum.

Fernand lifted the Swan from its loop around the scroll and carried it out to the showroom, rotating it so they could admire its shape, its flawless workmanship, and the grain of the wood. Then he handed the instrument to Claude and produced a chair and a bow. He signaled Sorel to silence the radio. "Is yours to play, M. Roselle."

Fernand was gracious while his partner stood glumly by. Claude understood that Baum had been deprived of a major commission. It was impossible to gauge the Swan's value on the open—or closed—market, because in recent years there'd been no comparable sales. The forma B celli of Stradivari's "Golden Period"—roughly 1707 to 1720—varied in terms of their varnish, how much of the original remained, how much wood had been replaced, and how well the instrument sounded. On all these counts the Silver Swan was, as Claude knew, impeccable, and the fact that he planned to keep it caused Baum a great loss. He had hoped, Claude guessed, to receive two or three million dollars as a commission on its sale.

Before he played, Claude studied the engravings of swans on either side of the scroll. He felt such intense joy he could barely lift the bow to the strings. But when he began the Bach Suite in C Major, the employees stopped work and gathered to listen. Francine watched with great satisfaction. When he finished playing, his small audience burst into applause.

Standing, he handed the cello back to the luthier. "Messieurs, do you think I might play the Swan next week, here at Alice Tully Hall? The sound is so much richer than my own instrument. I am already spoiled."

"*Anyone* who plays the Swan is after spoiled." Fernand laughed. "It makes everybody sound like a true virtuoso."

"I would need, of course, to come and practice every day until my hands adjusted. It would give me such pleasure to play the Swan in honor of the maestro at my first New York recital. Perhaps it's even not too late to say so in the program, I can ask my manager—and, of course, Mlle Feldmann as well."

"I repeat, M. Roselle," said the luthier, "it is after all your instrument to play. But we must make certain the insurance is in order before the Swan can leave the shop. Perhaps Heinrich will arrange it, yes? And you will remember that it comes back to us right after the concert, for adjustments I have promised not only to Alexandre Feldmann alive but now toward his memory. Until then, by all means, you may come and practice every day."

They said their farewells. Claude and Francine left the shop, he carrying his Tecchler. Both were elated as they parted in the busy street, Claude to rehearse with his pianist and Francine to go shopping a few blocks east at Bergdorf Goodman.

Claude walked downtown in a contemplative mood. He had treasured his visits with Alexander, who made it clear they could talk about anything and he would answer Claude's questions forthrightly. As Claude reached his teens, Alexander increasingly invited these tête-à-têtes. He would take Claude for long walks along Lake Lugano. Uninhibited, he would shock and delight his young companion with his frank opinions, advice, and risqué jokes and stories, none of which Claude would retell at home. Seeing them off on these excursions, Francine would admonish Alexander, "Don't fill his head with crazy ideas, Alexandre. We are not Americans." Alexander, of course, paid her no attention.

On one such walk, when Claude was about to enter the Tchaikovsky Competition for the first time, Alexander, who had come to coach him, asked, "So, young man, we've worked and worked on the cello performances. Now let me ask you how things are going with your romantic performances."

Claude, embarrassed and reticent, kicked a pebble along the path. "Oh come, come," Alexander persisted. "Certainly the young ladies must be after you. You're terribly handsome and quite the charmer."

"I'm not that much interested in girls," Claude answered seriously, "except in playing music with them, of course. I mean, I like girls very much, but Maman says I must concentrate on my cello and she thinks I'm too busy to go around with them."

"Is that what she says?" Alexander asked, a smile widening across his face. "You're not such a kid anymore, you know. At your age, I was living in New York City on my own and making love as often as I could get a girl into my bed."

"I think my parents would not approve of that, if they knew, M. Feldmann." Claude smiled. "I think we won't mention it to them."

"What else does your mother say on the subject?"

"She has very strong opinions—she says there is a right woman for every man, and I shall know when I find mine. She says also that one should save oneself for that woman, that marriage is sacred and, once married, one should remain true."

Alexander bellowed with laughter. Claude felt both hurt and puzzled. "Why do you laugh, M. Feldmann?"

Stopping short, Alexander turned to look at him and, studying his face, backtracked. "Not because your mother is wrong, of course. Just because it's so charmingly old-fashioned."

"What do *you* think?" Claude searched Alexander's face.

They continued walking. Clouds were gathering over the lake. "I think when one is young and full of energy and desire, one should enjoy it, enjoy the body and the pleasure, without sacrificing too much of one's work time. One should gather experience and then go back to the music, take all that experience back to the music. Take everything in your life back to the music. But the music must be the center of your life."

"Then why marry at all?" Claude asked. "Why not just continue having experiences, as you call them?"

"Because sooner or later you'll want not to be alone. You'll want someone to look after you."

"With music, you're never alone, M. Feldmann. Surely you believe that."

"Ah, but music does not dine with you or listen to you or make a family, and those are also important parts of life."

"I think I won't marry," Claude said, thoughtfully. "I have my mother and father for all those things you mention, and I like the idea of keeping my freedom."

"You'll feel that way till you meet the right woman, as your mother says, and want to keep her. Then you'll marry. But first, enjoy all the pleasures of youth."

❧

William Rossen lived in a new apartment complex in Chelsea, at the rear of the building. Facing west, his studio had additional soundproofing that permitted him to practice without disturbing the neighbors. He greeted Claude warmly at the door, telling him his wife and children were out for the afternoon, so they could rehearse in peace. Rossen, a much sought-after pianist, was a lanky man with a fringe of red hair and Vandyke beard. He had made his reputation as an accompanist and later embarked on a solo career. Ten years Claude's senior, he was doing him a favor. In New York, the name Rossen would fill a good-size concert hall, and to lend Roselle his imprimatur was to guarantee attention to Claude's debut.

Because they had played together only twice before, in Germany, they knew they had a great deal to do to prepare the Brahms sonatas—particularly the second. The Sonata in E Minor, op. 38, was familiar to them both, and they would also play the Violin Sonata No. 1 in G Major, op. 78, as arranged for cello and piano. But the third piece, the second Sonata for Piano and Violoncello in F Major, op. 99, was a major musical challenge. They had discussed it the night before.

In Rossen's living room, Claude opened his cello case and removed the bow and resin. He took out the music and then his Tecchler, feeling a twinge of disloyalty; the cello now seemed drab and pedestrian. It was as though his old companion—faithful and dependable—had been supplanted by something much more glamorous—a hausfrau replaced by a beautiful mistress. Claude told his host, in confidence, the news about the Silver Swan. Since he hoped to perform with it, it could not come as a surprise to Rossen when they walked onstage. The second movement in particular, Adagio affetuoso, offered him his best chance to show off the instrument's power.

His host, he could see, was impressed. "We always heard you were Feldmann's prize student. This certainly does prove it." The pianist studied him. "But why did it take you so long to play in America? I've often wondered."

"You know, my father never found it important to have a career here. He conducts only in Europe and seems to think it unnecessary to cross the Atlantic—perhaps because he was never *invited* to conduct in America and feels the insult deeply." Claude arranged his chair and music stand as he spoke. "And my mother, for reasons I don't understand, seemed determined to keep me away from the States. Of course I've traveled to New York before, but only a few times, as a tourist. It is, I must say, wonderful to finally come here to perform, and it's a great honor to play my first American concert with you, William. You've always accompanied much greater artists."

"Perhaps more famous," Rossen replied generously, "but not necessarily greater. Except, of course, for Alexander Feldmann, who was in a class by himself."

This gave Claude the opening he'd hoped for. "I've heard his daughter was also an exceptional talent. Do you know her?"

"I've met her, but I can't say I really know her. I heard her play several times. She was a remarkable performer. Her playing was special—something all her own, though you could hear her father's sensibility as well. She possessed virtuoso technique, but she never succumbed to melodrama or 'staginess,' just a melodic, reserved sensitivity and romanticism of tone. She had great integrity as a player and at the same time the ability to bewitch you. Real flamboyance, too, when it was appropriate. She was really something."

Claude said, after a moment, "And so gorgeous, it's hard not to notice her. Everything in one package for a great career."

They laughed.

"Have you any idea why she stopped concertizing?" Claude asked. "I'm so sorry not to have heard her."

"She made a few recordings, only a few, but they are extraordinary—the Dvořák in particular, and the Victor Herbert. The Haydn, too. Her pitch was true, I mean true like Greenwich mean time. And her ability to communicate with the listener was so profound as to be mysterious, but one never felt the effort behind it. You can still find them—the recordings. They're available and you should judge for yourself." The pianist paused, thoughtful. "As to why she ended her career, apparently she had tremendous performance anxiety and this grew worse instead of better. Finally, one night she collapsed onstage...that was in 2002, I believe."

"Stage fright," said Claude. "It's not something I've experienced. But I do know it can be devastating to a career." He paused. "I also heard rumors about an affair she had with Anton Pietovsky. Did you know anything about that?"

"It was impossible not to know about it. They were constant companions. Mariana was crazy about him. There was a lot of gossip, but I don't know what really happened. I do know his wife moved here from Moscow and Pietovsky gave Mariana up."

"Was her father upset? She was so young to be with someone Pietovsky's age, and he was married!"

"People said he didn't try to bring it to an end and he didn't stop being friends with Pietovsky after the affair broke up, even though Mariana was crushed. Strange man, Feldmann. Despite everything he said publicly about how brilliant a musician Mariana was and how she'd inherited his talent, he seemed to undermine rather than encourage her—to resent her success. He was rumored to be something of a tyrant, insisting she follow his musical ideas, complaining when she used a fingering that wasn't *his.* You know, that kind of thing. It is claimed that at the end of his life, the old man used her as a companion, a secretary and, virtually, a servant. She devoted herself to taking care of him. Many think Feldmann ruined her career."

Claude was intrigued. When the rehearsal was over, he would write a note to Mariana, inviting her to his concert, the reception, and dinner. Sensing that his mother would dislike the invitation, and remembering her behavior at breakfast, he decided not to tell her. Unlike his girlfriend, Sophie—so small and blond and compact, so Swiss and intellectual and self-contained—Mariana promised excitement. He had already found her phone number and address in the telephone book and carried it in his wallet. He was determined to know her better, and soon.

"Come, Claude, let's get to work." Rossen pulled out his piano bench. "We have a lot to accomplish before my brood returns."

CHAPTER THREE

Mariana

Mariana, distraught, fled from the lawyer's office back to the New York apartment she had leased to a friend during the years she'd lived with Alexander, and had now reclaimed. In the months since Alexander's death, he had nonetheless consumed her time and attention. She had buried him, mourned him, celebrated him, arranged memorials, made speeches, and done everything in her power to do what he would have wanted—what he had, in fact, expected her to do.

Now she felt pure boiling rage. Who the hell was Claude Roselle to get *her* cello? Alexander was a bastard. She had been so loyal, so foolish. He had cared for no one but himself and his own great legacy. Now, were it in her power, she would destroy that legacy. She felt humiliated. Everyone would know he had taken the Silver Swan away from her and given it to a stranger.

She blamed Francine Roselle. The woman had certainly schemed to get the cello for her son. Apparently, if she got nothing else out of their forty-odd-year relationship, she would get her son the damned instrument. Mariana remembered with revulsion Francine's attempt to embrace her in

Beecher's office and to inquire after her emotional state. She loathed the woman and wanted her to suffer.

Claude, though, had seemed genuinely surprised by the gift. He had behaved rather touchingly, Mariana decided, and she could not blame him. His perfidious mother had lived a lie that would hurt him if he ever found out. He, too, was a victim of their reckless, selfish liaison, whether he knew it or not.

Perhaps Claude's childhood had been as lonely as hers, she mused. Like her, he had been raised by parents who were consumed by their careers and love affairs. Neither she nor Claude had a sibling. Alexander had frequently said to her, "You don't need a sibling, you have the Swan. Look how she sits next to you in the backseat! And she doesn't quarrel!" Although she was fiercely proud that her family owned such a treasure, she had also resented this favored sibling who traveled everywhere with Alexander. The Swan flew only first-class on airplanes and toured the capitals of Europe, which Mariana longed to see. She and Pilar stayed home.

Mariana had attended her father's departures, standing just inside their apartment, holding the door for him. Maxxi, their cocker spaniel, would start whining piteously the moment her master lifted his suitcase and cello and brought them to the foyer. And after Alexander's departure, the dog would slink off to curl herself into a corner of his studio, whimpering.

Pilar herself would not come to the door. Alexander, going to the dinette to find her, tried to kiss her goodbye and Mariana would see her mother turn her face away. Then he would sweep past Mariana, giving her a hug and a pat on the head, grabbing his bag, coat, and cello. He would tell her to be a good girl and remind her to practice.

"Take care of your mother," he would always say, as the elevator door closed. And although she had been proud to have this task assigned her, she had no idea, in the face of her mother's stark anger and grief, how best to fulfill it.

It was as if her mother's fragile inner light dialed down, as if her husband had controlled a human dimmer switch. Pilar would sit at the table, smoking and making interconnecting circles on the borders of the *New York Post* with the stub of a pencil.

Sometimes Mariana tried to cheer her up, to propose a plan—a visit to Pilar's father in Queens, a shopping trip to Macy's, or a stop for cream cheese on date-nut bread sandwiches at Chock Full o' Nuts. She could see her mother was suffering and she suffered too, as much from her mother's pain as from the departure that caused it. She knew that her mother, while Alexander was away, had little to do and few friends to see. And yet she seemed to get no pleasure from Mariana's afternoon return from school. She did not rise from her chair or prepare a snack or ask how her day had been. "Do you have a lot of homework?" was the most she asked. The only traces of her day's activity were the filled ashtray, the phone messages she took for Alexander on a pad at her elbow, and the evidence of a trip to the newsstand to get the paper—these and the books, the stacks of Modern Library editions, which grew around her chair.

"Mama, I'm supposed to ask you if you'd like to volunteer to work at the school bazaar this year. It's on Saturday, April 7th."

"Tell them I can't, please. Your father will just be coming home." Pilar always knew Alexander's schedule, but only the dates of his departures and returns, never where he was on any given day. For this information, Mariana had to consult the engagement book on the desk. She checked the itinerary daily and left herself little clues as to whether her mother had opened it. She rarely did.

"I think it would be fun," Mariana persisted. "I like it when you come to school." She couldn't remember the last time Pilar had made such a visit. Her friends' mothers were always buzzing around the PTA office, working to raise money for some cause or charity at the expensive little private school, Wide World, which dearly held to its pretensions to a social conscience.

"I'm not particularly fond of the other mothers," Pilar answered. "They wear full-length mink coats and insist their maids work twelve hours a day while they take taxis to school, raise money for protest marches and the Fresh Air Fund, and let their children go home alone every afternoon to household help."

Mariana thought it might be nice to have a welcoming maid to greet her at the door and set out a snack. She was surprised by her mother's contemptuous tone. "The maids are there," Mariana clarified, "and some of them are really friendly. We're not alone."

The Feldmanns didn't employ a maid. It was against her mother's principles and they didn't have the money for it. Payments on the purchase of the Swan still claimed their funds. Mariana often chose to visit her friends after school, dreading the return to her own silent apartment. But she couldn't stay long because of her practice schedule. At home, with Pilar ever-present, she felt most alone. "Anyway, if you feel that way, why did you and Papa send me to Wide World?"

"I thought it would be truer to its principles. God knows what your father thought."

"Did he visit it with you? Did you choose it together?"

"No. He didn't have the time or interest."

Mariana asked again, wistfully. "Well, anyway, I wish you'd work at the bazaar."

Pilar lit a cigarette and took up her pencil again. "I'll speak to your father about it if he calls. You know Saturdays are his busy teaching day and he needs me here."

"Okay. Thanks, Mama."

⁂

Mariana had heard Alexander speak with pride of her mother's principles, of her work as founding director of a ballet school that fostered the talents of poor children, of her social work. To do this, she had given up her position in the corps of the New York City Ballet. Like her parents, Pilar had been ardently against social injustice and privilege. She had gone south in the early days of the civil rights movement and championed racial equity in the arts. She'd taught in settlement houses and clubs, in public schools in poor neighborhoods. Alexander told people how hard he'd had to struggle to capture her attention, so committed was she to her school and what he called "her Socialist ideals." (This was not exactly true, Mariana later discovered; her mother, very much in love, had waited several years while Alexander made up his mind to marry her.)

"But Papa, why does she only stay home?" Mariana had once asked.

"Because she *has* to look after you," he said, "and she *wants* to look after me. My career makes many demands on her. I need her to be home when I return from tours and you need her to be home when I'm away on tours." He looked as if this explained everything, and when she still seemed puzzled, he said with exasperation, "It was no longer suitable for her to be working with those people. I asked her to give it up when you were born. It just wasn't practical anymore for her to have so many commitments that conflicted with my own schedule."

Her mother's anger washed over Mariana, the bystander, and scared her. She tried to understand how her mother could love her father so passionately and protectively, craving his attention and devoting her life to him, while at the same time resenting his success and raging at his absence. When Alexander returned, Pilar would always punish him, but he would slowly coax her back out of the darkness. Once, winking at Mariana, he confided, "She and Maxxi are the same in this; they have their pride. They must, with patience, be brought around."

❧

On the morning after Mariana returned from Boston, her doorbell rang and a delivery man handed her a bouquet of flowers. She ripped open the envelope. The note came from Claude:

Dear Mariana,

I hope you do not find it forward that I am writing to you after our last encounter. I'm giving a concert at Alice Tully Hall this Saturday, playing Brahms with William Rossen. It is my first New York recital and I would be honored, truly delighted, if you would be my guest at the concert and the reception and dinner afterward, given by Edith Libbey. I feel we have so many reasons to know each other, to be friends. I hope you'll agree to come. I'll leave a ticket for you at the box office, in any event, and will ask Mrs. Libbey to send you an invitation.

With fond regards,

Claude

She felt a rush of excitement that conflicted violently with the anguish she'd been feeling since her departure from Boston. Had she hoped to hear from Claude? Many years had passed since her last, and only serious, involvement with a man, Anton Pietovsky. It had not turned out as she hoped; he left her.

Removing the paper and ribbon from the bouquet, she admired the extravagance of the arrangement, the largesse of the gesture, and the scent of the fresh spring flowers. She did not even have a vase to hold so many blooms, but she brought her largest glass pitcher from the kitchen and pressed them in. Pietovsky had made such gifts—flowers awaited her in every greenroom, chocolates and champagne at her hotels, an ermine shawl to wrap around her gowns in winter, and on her thirtieth birthday, a diamond bracelet. He was a romantic. Perhaps Claude was too. Or maybe he just felt guilty.

She set the flowers on a table that still held a photo of herself with Anton and her father, a large framed black-and-white picture, taken in 1989. She had been seventeen and eager to meet the sensational Russian conductor, fifteen years her father's junior, who had recently engaged Feldmann to play the Dvořák concerto under his baton, in Moscow. In the photo, Alexander, as usual, towers over the group; Pilar is behind the camera. Anton has his arm around Mariana, who has already emerged as a beauty, taller than he. They are in New York at her parents' apartment, just about to have a celebratory dinner party. Behind them, the table is set.

Mariana remembered the occasion vividly. Anton had been barely able to speak English, though his attempts were unselfconscious, voluble, and full of large gesticulation. When Mariana entered the dining room, she took note of the two empty bottles of Russian vodka on the table, making rings on the cloth. The two men had apparently been long engaged in drinking and talking music in Alexander's studio. She looked at the conductor, whom she'd heard so much about, and found something quite appealing, something alive and endearing in the way he came toward her and kissed both her cheeks, called her Marushka as he held her head in his hands. Her father was beaming.

"Ah," Pietovsky cried, pressing her against his wrinkled Russian peasant shirt, "now I have met beautiful daughter about so much I have heard. I give her one more hug." He did. "You must, Sashinka, pour her some vodka before is gone. Is my gift," he explained to Mariana, "straight from steppes." Alexander poured the viscous liquid into a small glass and handed it to her.

"Now here is how is done," Pietovsky explained, as he linked his arm with hers, holding his own glass, and threw the vodka down his throat. She smiled and tried to take a sip. "No, no sip," he bellowed. "Whole thing." She did it. Her eyes teared.

"Now we do again," he insisted. "This time we toast each other, our friendship." Mariana didn't want any more vodka, but her father poured another glass and handed it to her. So once again she linked arms and, attempting more enthusiasm, tossed the vodka down as did the eager Pietovsky. While he leaned against her side, he continued his conversation with Alexander about the great Russian cellist, Rostropovich. "Is amazing, Sasha, how he can remember every note first time he plays it. I test him a few times. He never fails. Is a great gift — such remembering. Do you have it?" he asked Mariana, turning to her.

"Yes, yes she does," Alexander said with pride. Mariana looked at him quizzically. She had no such gift or photographic memory but understood that her father wanted to promote her talent.

"Good for you, darling," the conductor said. "I like to test you too." He smiled cheerfully and kissed her again. "You come play with my orchestra. After your papa."

"I would be very honored, Maestro," she replied. "If you think I'm ready..."

"No, I am not maestro — such nonsense. I am your Anton, your friend, your papa's friend and your mama's. We must drink to that."

Pilar, appearing from the kitchen, whispered to Mariana, "I think you've had enough. Throw the next one over your shoulder at the wall."

"Why don't I just say no thank you?"

"Your father doesn't want to offend the maestro. He feels very flattered to have him here. We can wash the wall later." Mariana, watching Pilar place candles on the table, couldn't believe her mother was encouraging her to throw liquor on the charcoal walls.

As they waited for other guests to arrive, the Russian drew her to the Steinway to expound on the piece she told him she was working on, Tchaikovsky's Rococo Variations. An accomplished pianist, he played the accompaniment and sang the cello part from memory. He too had an extraordinary ability to retain music, so important to a conductor. Mariana felt charmed by his warmth and the eager attention he lavished upon her. Pilar was in the kitchen with the Russian cook they'd hired for the occasion, overseeing the menu. Alexander fussed at the bar, opening bottles and bringing ice. Mariana invited Pietovsky to sit with her on the couch while they talked about the cello repertoire and which pieces she felt she'd mastered. He leaned toward her and commented on the scent she was wearing. "Lilac," she said, smiling, "my favorite."

"Ah, this I won't forget, I shall bring you lilac when you play for me." He took her hand and stroked it. "What instrument are you playing?"

"A Vuillaume," she answered, "a copy of my father's cello."

"I must hear you play. Bring the Vuillaume to my hotel. I shall be here for some days more."

"If you telephone me, I'll come," she answered, arranging her dress and moving slightly farther away. She would ask her father if he thought it a good idea.

The doorbell rang and she rose to answer it. The guests began to arrive, mostly Russians, in Pietovsky's honor—old friends of his. The party grew louder, full of bonhomie and laughter and Russian jokes Mariana didn't understand but enjoyed in any case because it was such a pleasure to see her mother presiding over the table and looking happy. Always, Pietovsky stayed at Mariana's side. He was lionized and toasted over and over again, asked about conditions in the Soviet Union now that the government was tumbling, questioned about whether he would now come to live in America with his wife, the famous Soviet actress, and their daughters.

My God, Mariana thought, for such a famous conductor, he is so friendly and without self-importance.

"Aha," he answered this last question. "First I see if I want my wife so close." Everyone laughed. He looked at Mariana, eyes twinkling. "I see beauty here all around me. Maybe is better if wife stays in Moscow."

Mariana looked quickly at her father. He was watching her intently, and she couldn't tell what he was thinking. To his old friend Zena Padrova, a well-known Russian cellist, Alexander called out, "Tell him, Zena, about how she plays the cello — what an artist she is, even at such a young age."

Zena took control of the conversation, sparkling. "Anton, parents always brag about their children, but you must know, Mariana is already much greater talent than her father, or just as good as he was at her age. I think you will be amazed if she ever agrees to play for you."

"Oh, she will," Alexander answered on her behalf. "She is already playing all over the world."

"Do you travel alone?" Pietovsky asked, surprised.

"Almost always," Mariana answered, "but I'm met, of course, wherever I go."

When the evening finally came to an end, the wall behind Mariana was streaked with vodka shots, although the other guests had been less wasteful. Pietovsky could hardly stand up, he'd had so much to drink. He slouched against the closet door with his eyes shut as Pilar produced his fur coat.

"I think you'd best stay with us tonight, Anton," Alexander said, taking his arm. Pilar glared at him. "I'll put him to bed in my studio," Alexander assured her, "and take him to his hotel in the morning. Look, he can't even walk." Sensing conflict, Mariana hastily left the foyer and went toward her room. Turning back, she saw Pietovsky watching her over her father's shoulder. He winked.

Late that night, he found his way to her room and crawled into her bed. He was in his underwear and reeked of alcohol. She didn't want to cry out. He lay alongside her, running his hands over her body, murmuring, "Such beautiful girl, Mariana. I want you. I want to eat you, I want to fuck you." He soon fell asleep, drooling on her pillow.

She placed a metal wastebasket next to the bed and crept out to the living room couch, taking his sable coat from the closet, wrapping it around her, and pulling it over her head. Early in the morning, she moved to her father's studio and curled up on the couch Pietovsky had abandoned the night before. He left with her father to return to his hotel. Perhaps he was embarrassed or forgetful, but he never called to have her come to play for him. And she didn't encounter the maestro again until eight years later when he attended her first recital in Moscow.

❧

Mariana sat at her desk in the living room and looked at Claude's flowers. She considered whether she would attend his concert and whether she could bear to encounter his mother again, to witness the spectacle of her triumph. She felt so painfully Alexander's disloyalty, the punishment he had dealt her for failing to live up to his expectations, the final lacerating blow to what remained of her fragile sense that he had ever loved her. He had waited until he extracted every last drop of her devotion. Then, dying, he had delivered the coup de grâce.

The warming light of early spring greeted Mariana as she stepped out of her building and crossed the park. She walked briskly to Fifth Avenue and turned south, weaving among the baby strollers, single and double, pushed by young mothers and nannies on cell phones. Clusters of children in uniforms, coming home from East Side private schools, jostled her as they walked, teasing and shouting, excited by the newly warm weather. As she approached the Guggenheim, the crowd thickened with tourists speaking the mélange of languages so frequently heard in New York. She walked along the park, smelling the dank earth now coming back to life. Navigating the throngs of people surging in and out of the Metropolitan Museum, she thought about Claude's invitation and hoped there was more to it than mere politesse.

After Anton left her, she had never again sought a relationship. Only seduction aroused strong feelings of desire in her—the man who appeared backstage after a concert to escort her to the reception, the technician in the recording studio, the stranger at a party, the lover who belonged to someone else. She wanted no more.

Alexander had schooled her in the feckless nature of men, and she had believed him. Men were adversaries whom she was challenged to beat at their own game. She made them want her and let them believe they had her, without ever letting herself be drawn in, sewn up, owned. Until Anton, she'd always slipped away in the end, returning to her Vuillaume and her career.

Leaning on the mottled stone wall bordering Central Park, she watched children running about the playground, swinging and digging and sliding. The riotous noise and laughter amused her. Kids were adorable. She enjoyed her friends' children up to a point. But she'd never wanted her own. Perhaps the biological clock everyone talked about would kick in; she was only thirty-eight. There was still time for an unexpected change of heart. Even the thought made her smile, it was so improbable.

She walked on, heading for Bergdorf Goodman. The lush scents of perfumes and unguents enveloped her as she entered the store, a relief from the omnipresent smell of horse manure around the Plaza. She wandered around the first floor, enjoying the luxurious bazaar, touching and smelling, and remembering with a shiver the days when she'd slipped costume jewelry into her bag, unnoticed, just for the thrill. Now, however, she intended to treat herself to the whole deal—the lingerie, the Zanotti stilettos, the new evening bag, scent. After all, she reasoned, what were credit cards for? She would buy the sexiest dress in the place. This time, she wouldn't need the full, billowing skirt required for playing the cello. She would get something bone-clinging and gorgeous for Claude to peel away with his long fingers.

❧

On the night of the concert, she put on the dress, a deep purple cylinder of watered taffeta, with a plunging décolleté. She wore her mother's amethyst choker, small diamond studs she'd bought for herself on tour in Poland, and a black velvet cape. On her wrist, she clasped the diamond bracelet Anton had given her on her thirtieth birthday. She had pinned her dark hair into a swirling French twist; strands were already falling about her face as she got out of the taxi in front of Tully Hall. People on the plaza asked for tickets to the concert: SOLD OUT was plastered across the poster in front. In her new and highest heels, she was taller than most of the crowd in the lobby, and heads turned toward her as she arrived, sweeping in on a gust of warm wind. The moment Mariana entered, she recognized familiar faces. It seemed to her the whole cello world had come to hear the Swiss virtuoso's debut. People waved at her. Some pressed her hand. Several who had not attended any Feldmann memorial service condoled with her. Others asked how well she knew Roselle.

Heinrich Baum approached and embraced her warmly. "It has been too long since we've seen each other, my dear. I am pleased to have your father's cello in the shop." His German accent was faint. "But it is much more pleasing still to see his other treasure."

"Flatterer," she said, leaning down to brush her lips against his cheek.

"No, Mariana, I tell you the truth. Like the Stradivarius, you grow more beautiful each year."

She answered, "Three hundred years from now, I might amount to something," and he laughed. Then they spoke about Alexander, and Baum told her how much he was missed at Baum & Fernand, how gratified he would have been at Tully Hall this evening to hear his protégé play Brahms. "And think, my dear, how kind death was to him—it came so suddenly, without suffering." As the lobby lights signaled the concert would start and the crowd advanced into the hall, Baum took her arm and murmured, "But how shocking the news about the Swan. We have both lost a very great deal. We must meet and talk." Then he turned away.

Mariana settled in her seat: fourth row center, facing the cellist's unoccupied chair. She noticed, one row ahead and to the right, Francine sitting with old friends of Alexander's, the

Kappelmans. The lights flickered twice, then dimmed. After a long silence, when the audience had settled down, Claude stepped briskly onto the stage, wearing a tuxedo and a dark gray dress shirt. He held a cello in one hand, a bow in the other. William Rossen followed, and the two men bowed to each section of the audience. Claude's smile was wide and his face radiated confidence as he acknowledged the extended applause. With a well-practiced flourish, he sat down, twirling the cello and placing it between his knees. She looked up at him. His chair faced her, his cello caught the light. It glowed a deep auburn gold. The volute scroll glittered and shone. Mariana gasped. Not twenty feet away, the soloist bent his curly head as if in prayer, then raised his eyes again and, glancing at Rossen, lifted his bow. He played the Silver Swan.

CHAPTER FOUR

Claude

Having played his final encore, an elated Claude retired to the greenroom. A line of men and women stood waiting in the corridor. The room itself was mobbed. People filed forward for the chance to meet him, praise him, and ask him to autograph their programs or take a photograph together or sign one of his CDs. Across the room, William Rossen also shook hands and talked animatedly. Francine stood close to Claude, flushed with pride, speaking to his admirers as they moved on. Drenched in sweat, Claude removed the jacket of his tuxedo and draped a towel around his neck. Laughing, embracing them often, he leaned down to greet his admirers, speaking a mixture of languages. A laurel would have suited him tonight. He had played impeccably and had nothing to regret, no phrase to revisit. Now he could relax.

Heinrich Baum arrived backstage to relieve him of the Stradivarius. Baum held the cello in the corner next to its case, showing off the instrument and speaking of its history. Several people asked him what would now become of the Swan and, by prior agreement with the Roselles, Baum replied, "It is not yet decided. Or anyhow, I've not yet been informed." Claude, over his mother's objection, had insisted that the news of his good fortune not be revealed until he spoke with Mariana, if she *would* speak with him, and there had not been sufficient time to change the printed program. Therefore, no announcement had been made as to his ownership of the Silver Swan. When he received the message from Mariana, accepting his invitation, he told himself he would play for both Alexander and his daughter. Her presence in the hall would validate his own.

Slowly, the greenroom emptied out, leaving only Rossen, the Roselles, and Heinrich Baum, who was taking the instrument back to the safe in his office. "I expect to hear from you before you leave on tour," the dealer said as he fastened the case. "We have arrangements to make with Pierre. Can you come by the shop tomorrow?" Claude was more than willing. As Baum went down the corridor, Claude turned to William Rossen. "I can't thank you enough," he said, clasping the pianist's arm.

"We must do it again, eh? It was a pleasure to work together."

"I'll ask my manager to be in touch with yours. Let's get them to arrange some future dates. Next year, perhaps? The season after that?"

"By all means." Rossen looked at his watch. "But now we're late for the Libbey reception. We should get going. As you know, I have two young kids and they get up early on Sundays. No chance of sleeping in..."

"You go ahead. We'll follow in a few minutes."

Claude changed his shirt and combed his hair. His mother helped him into his coat. "Tell me honestly, Maman, what did you think—you who are my sternest judge? What will you tell Papa?"

She laughed and reached up to kiss his cheek. "I'll tell him you were a triumph and that you gave me the greatest joy I've felt in a long time."

"Good," Claude said. "Then I'm happy." He paused, frowning. "Except, I have one worry—I haven't seen Mariana. She didn't come to the greenroom. Do you think something's wrong?"

Francine's expression changed. "You invited her to the reception. Surely she'll attend, she is not rude. You mustn't worry so much about her. We hardly know her, and only difficulties can arise out of knowing her better at this point. It's all too complicated with the cello."

"But wouldn't her father have wanted us to extend ourselves to her? Isn't that why he brought us together?"

"Come, let's get to the party. I'm quite sure you'll find her there, *chéri*. Your hosts await you."

❧

At eleven, Claude and Francine arrived at the Jumeirah-Essex House. As they entered the lobby, Francine, looking around, complained that the Essex House had been bought by Arabs since her last visit, and ruined. "It is tarted up."

Claude hushed her. "We're not supposed to say such things, Maman. This is America."

She shrugged. "Well, it's true. Look at this lobby."

Their host, Mrs. Edith Libbey, had inherited a large fortune. Widowed by a banker, she possessed an important art collection. Sophie knew of it and she had told Claude to keep his eyes open. "It is legendary," she'd said, urging him to pay attention on her behalf and make a full report. "I wish I could be there with you."

"Why not?" he had asked. "You could come for the weekend, just for the New York recital."

"You know I can't. That weekend it's impossible." It was her mother's sixtieth birthday, a celebration she could not miss.

"I do know that. And I promise to report on everything I see." Now, hoping to spend time with Mariana, he was relieved she hadn't come.

Mrs. Libbey occupied the penthouse. The elevator man consulted a list of invited guests and took them up. During the long ride, he stood with his white-gloved hands folded in front of him, saying not a word. When the doors opened, they stepped directly into the foyer of the Libbey apartment and were greeted by their hostess. Mrs. Libbey, a tiny, brittle woman with bright eyes—the only things that seemed to move in a face immobilized by decades of plastic surgery—shook their hands. Everything about her person seemed like tinder—papery, vulnerable to a passing spark. She greeted Francine familiarly, then complimented Claude on his performance and told him how much solace she had found in music since her husband died.

"I often stay up here in my little aerie for days at a time, listening to music. You must have a look 'round at the art. Your mother too might like to revisit the paintings. Mr. Feldmann was most fond of them. It gave him such pleasure to look when he visited. I hope you will also find it interesting, Claude, if I may call you that? A musician must be sensitive to the visual arts. I always enjoyed that about your mentor."

A butler appeared behind her, dressed as formally as Claude himself, inquiring what they wished to drink. Claude asked for a very dry martini, and his mother a glass of red wine. Edith Libbey escorted them down three carpeted steps into an enormous room with windows facing north over Central Park. As they entered, everyone stopped talking. "And here, at last," proclaimed Mrs. Libbey in her whispery voice, "is our guest of honor. I'm sure you'll agree he's been too long in crossing the pond to offer us his talent."

Claude smiled, puzzled. This was an expression he had not heard before: "the pond." He would remember it. The guests applauded and resumed their conversations. Mrs. Libbey gave the Roselles a chance to admire the view. To Francine, she said, "I'm very glad to see you looking so well. It's been years since I've had the pleasure of entertaining you and Alexander. How very sad that he's no longer with us, but at ninety, one must expect the end to come." Looking heavenward, she said, "Soon it will be my turn."

"I doubt it," Claude said quickly. "You're not old enough, surely."

She smiled at him for the first time, pleased. "One can never count on anything after the age of seventy."

"Well, then, you have a long period of certainty ahead."

His mother, out of Mrs. Libbey's line of sight, rolled her eyes.

Edith Libbey smiled again. "I will ask my secretary, Carol, to show you my collection. Meanwhile, please make the acquaintance of those guests you have not met. We are sixteen tonight at our midnight supper, and now that everyone is here, I must consult with my chef." In tiny, hurried steps, she crossed the room and disappeared through carved wooden doors.

Claude and Francine separated to greet the other guests. They knew William Rossen, of course, and Claude's concert manager. People were drinking, talking, and plucking hors d'oeuvres off trays passed by the catering staff. As he circulated, Claude looked for Mariana. He caught a glimpse of her in shadow at the far end of the room. Leaning against the window with a drink in her hand, staring down at the glittering city, she seemed very much alone. Her rigid posture, turned away from the other guests, did not invite conversation. Relieved to know she had come after all, Claude had to shift his attention to a man at his elbow, who introduced himself as a board member of Lincoln Center.

"Congratulations," said the man—Claude did not catch his name. "You did yourself—did all of us—proud. I so admire the Brahms sonatas."

"Yes, they are marvels, aren't they? Was the program overlong?"

"Not for this member of the audience. Had he written another piece for cello and piano, I would have welcomed it too. Brahms was a pianist, of course—I needn't tell you that—but he understood the cello, didn't he? He had, or so it seems to me, a particular sympathy for the cello's register—I needn't tell you that either—and the sonatas are among his most simpatico works..."

As soon as he was able to disengage himself, Claude walked toward Mariana, coming up behind her and looking over her shoulder at the view. His face reflected back in the window, as did hers. He could smell the delicate fragrance she wore.

She was silent as she took a step forward and turned her face toward his. Their eyes met for several moments before Claude moved back and smiled at her. "You are as lovely as your father always said you were." Still, she said nothing. "Tell me, Mariana, did you approve of my playing tonight? I felt I was playing in your father's memory, to honor him. And I was also playing for you, knowing you were there. It matters very much to me what you thought."

"Yes, my father would have approved," she said coolly. "Apparently, he was immensely proud of you." Now she dropped her eyes and took a sip of her drink.

"Ah, do you say that because he gave me the Silver Swan or because he spoke of me?"

"My father spoke almost exclusively about himself."

Disappointed but unfazed, Claude told himself she wasn't being truthful. He was confident that he had had a privileged relationship with Alexander Feldmann and had earned his teacher's esteem.

"I see your mother's here with you." Mariana was mocking. "Is your father in town also?"

"No, my father didn't come. He has his own busy schedule, and because I play so many concerts, he follows my career much less closely than my mother does." He laughed. "Besides, my father is so Eurocentric, he doesn't feel a concert in New York is as important as any I play in a European capital! Were I to be playing the Dvořák concerto with the New York Philharmonic, he still wouldn't come. He just doesn't like America."

"It seems your mother does not share his opinion."

"She would go everywhere with me if I allowed her to. She hasn't enough to do these days. But sometimes I prefer the company of women *other* than my mother."

Pursuing what he hoped was his advantage, he continued, "And I like you very much, Mariana. You are a beautiful woman."

She put her empty glass on the window ledge and looked away.

Claude took her hand. "Did it make you terribly sad to see the Swan in the hands of someone other than your father tonight?"

"I knew it would happen one day." She paused. "But I always believed I would be the one to choose who that cellist would be."

"And are you disappointed in his choice?"

She again looked at him intensely without answering. Behind them, a woman appeared.

"Here you are! I'm Carol, Mrs. Libbey's secretary. She asked me to show you around the apartment, to introduce you to her art. It's a very special collection."

Carol was in her fifties—trim, and brisk. She extended her hand. Claude drew Mariana along with him, saying, "We'd be delighted." Carol turned back to inquire, "Should we invite your mother to join us? She always loved these paintings."

"That isn't necessary," Claude answered. "I understand she's been here several times before with Alexander Feldmann. Let's just be the three of us." Looking back, as he tightened his grip on Mariana's hand, he saw grief in her deep, dark eyes.

❧

The apartment was vast. They moved from room to room, astonished at what they saw. Claude remembered Sophie's request. He thought he should write things down to tell her about on the phone. But with Mariana so close, he didn't much care to. It was hard to conjure Sophie here, her earnest, young face, polished and pure in the way of well-brought-up

Swiss young women. He stood close to Mariana, keeping his fingers in contact with the fabric of her dress as he guided her from room to room. They were shown important paintings — an oil portrait of a princess by Hans Holbein the Younger, a series of Raphael drawings, a shelf of Cycladic sculpture, a library from Venice with a set of Canalettos, a Whistler, a John Singer Sargent, and two beach scenes by Winslow Homer which, Carol told them, Mr. Libbey had particularly loved.

"He was from Maine; they had a place on Soames Sound. I myself barely knew him — he was dying by the time I came to work here — but he always said that Homer *spoke* to him."

Mariana was silent. She hugged her waist. Claude stared at her, pretending to look at the art on the walls but studying her profile and the plunging purple neckline. She yielded and leaned toward him.

There were portraits of ancestral Libbeys — wearing white ruffled shirts and black coats. There was a dancer by Degas, a decoupage by Matisse. Carol discoursed at wearying length about who bought which picture when, and from which dealer, and where.

A butler approached, half bowing. "Ladies and gentlemen, dinner is served."

In the dining room, an ornate crystal-and-gold chandelier sparkled above the table, and antique gold sconces hung between paintings of flowers: Renoir and Fantin-Latour. The table had been set with sumptuous linens, a silver service fit for giants, crystal goblets, and elaborate china whose floral pattern reflected the theme of the oils. As they entered the dining room, Carol withdrew before they had a chance to thank her.

The Roselles were shown to places flanking Mrs. Libbey, who already sat at the table's head, diminutive in her tall thronelike chair. She had a frozen smile on her face and a large halo of immovable blond hair. Claude was not happy that Mariana had been seated at the other end of the table; there could be no further conversation. At least he could watch her, perhaps catch her eye from time to time. He wondered if she had wanted to sit beside him. Mrs. Libbey leaned toward him. Across the table, at Francine's right, sat the famous Russian cellist Zena Padrova, now in her eighties. Long retired from the stage, she was widely respected as a teacher. He recognized her at once. He had seen her embrace Mariana just before they sat down to dinner. Feldmann had told Claude riotous stories about Padrova. She was boisterous, bawdy, and full of a vital and irrepressible life force Feldmann cherished. Claude could see she must have been very attractive. She had already embarked on telling a joke—"And I told him, not again!" Her companions laughed.

Mrs. Libbey called the table to order and thanked her guests for coming, then proposed a toast: "*An die Musik!*" and "To our honored guests."

As she finished, Claude rose to thank their hostess for the party and the meal to come. He lifted his glass to her, then turned toward Mariana, raising it slightly higher as his eyes met hers.

The dinner began. Servers, wielding silver trays, rushed in and out with *saumon en gelée*, a rack of lamb, a puree of walnuts, and a tray of glistening roasted vegetables. This elaborate meal had been described, in the invitation, as a simple postconcert supper. But then, Claude remembered with amusement, Mrs. Libbey had described the apartment as her "little aerie." Her sense of proportion had obviously failed her. This might be, he reflected, either a condition of age or a condition of wealth.

Now Mrs. Libbey locked her gaze upon Claude and would not release him. His mother did not help at all. She was deeply engaged in a conversation with Zena Padrova about Alexander. Claude wished he could hear what they said, they spoke so intensely. He glanced across the table from time to time, as he politely answered Mrs. Libbey's questions: yes, he still lived in Lugano, yes he admired the Villa Serbelloni in Bellagio and of course the Villa d'Este. At one moment, he noticed that his mother's eyes had filled with tears and Mme Padrova was offering her napkin. Claude could not imagine what they might be saying. His mother rarely cried in his presence, but after Feldmann's death she had often wiped tears from her cheeks. "It's hard," she would say, "to lose such an old friend. You'll see one day. One feels so alone."

At the other end of the table, Claude observed Mariana chatting easily, laughing, and allowing the waiters to fill her wineglass again and again. At one point, she told a story about her father—his time in Prades with Pablo Casals and how he had annoyed the maestro by flirting with the village girls and taking them on picnics atop Mont Canigou. Everyone roared with laughter. She was not shy, nor did she lack self-confidence. And she resolutely would not meet his eyes again.

As they finished dessert, William Rossen asked if anyone had noticed that the floral arrangements on the table mysteriously matched those in the paintings. "Ah, you have discovered my secret!" Mrs. Libbey exclaimed, clapping her hands. "I always wait to see if anyone will notice. The florist has standing instructions to make a Renoir and Fantin-Latour. It is my little test, and, sir, tonight, you win."

They applauded the pianist and studied the beautiful flowers—on both the table and walls. With that, Mrs. Libbey stood up and made it clear she was weary, quite ready for them to depart. Claude looked at his watch. It was two a.m.

At the elevator door, he went to Mariana and said, "I have a week in New York, before I start my tour. I would like to know you better, Mariana. I feel our lives have become entwined, thanks to the Swan and all the other things we share. Would you have dinner with me tomorrow?"

"The three of us?" She looked at him intently.

Standing closer, he whispered, as his mother approached. "No. I'll make a reservation for two wherever you choose."

Now she did not hesitate. "Cafe Luxembourg at seven thirty."

"Thank you, Mariana. *À demain.*"

CHAPTER FIVE

Mariana

Leaving the party at two fifteen, Mariana tipped the hotel doorman who hailed her cab, and threw herself back against the vinyl seat. "The bastard," she muttered several times, "the absolute bastard." The cabdriver, alarmed, looked at her in the rearview mirror. She gave him her address. How clear it was that Francine Roselle had often been in America with Alexander—and that they had shared friends and restaurants and possibly even hotels many times in the city. And he had written that she *never* came here. The lies—even as he wrote his last letter to her.

Had he truly loved anyone? She could think of only one person Alexander had treated with absolute respect and tenderness. That was his own mother, her grandmother Rosa. He had been devoted to her. When Rosa was alive, they would travel, as a family, to visit her in the nursing home in Albany, for which Alexander paid. They saw her as often as his hectic schedule allowed. Driving up from the city on the thruway, they stayed only for the afternoon. Mariana had felt sad and frightened in the nursing home. Old people in wheelchairs in the corridors clamored for her attention or slept with their toothless mouths hanging open. Rosa herself was alert and sharp of mind, though she had gone blind in her late eighties. "All that knitting she did in her youth, in poor light," Alexander complained angrily to Pilar. "My father kept her at it to raise capital for his business."

Alexander would sit at his mother's side, holding her hand, telling her about his concerts and reading aloud his reviews. Always, when it was time to go, Rosa's sightless eyes would fill with tears. Alexander would tell her exactly when he could come again and she would always answer, "With luck, I'll still be here." Perhaps he really had cherished his mother, Mariana thought. But she wasn't sure.

❧

The morning after the concert, she slept late. Exhausted when she came home, she had kicked off her shoes and thrown her gown onto the small chair in the corner. It slipped to the floor, a mountain of taffeta. The slanting morning sunlight that briefly lit the room had moved on by the time she awoke. Her bedroom could barely contain the queen-size bed she'd bought when she returned from Swann's Way after Alexander's death. Over her head hung a painting from her parents' apartment, the only one Alexander had been willing to part with when Pilar died. The Chaim Gross landscape had been her mother's favorite—a gift from Gross's widow, an old friend. She reached for her bedside lamp, switched it on, and looked at the clock. Eleven thirty.

She thought about the way Claude had come up behind her at the party. He was brash, seductive, and self-confident—qualities she'd always found irresistible. She liked to be touched by an attractive man before she had given permission. At the window the night before, she had stepped backward and pressed herself against him. She could feel him stiffen. Seeing his face reflected in the glass, she had almost turned to kiss him. She'd felt wild and out of control, though she had remained cool to him. Now, conjuring him in her mind, her breath quickened. She ran her hands over her naked body, under the covers. After a while, she made herself get out of bed to make coffee.

Claude would carry the Swan back to Switzerland after Fernand finished the restoration. He had told her this. She wondered how long it would take Fernand to do his work. Was it possible she would never play it again? She couldn't let that happen. Seized with longing, she picked up the phone and called Baum & Fernand to make an appointment.

That afternoon, Mariana took the subway downtown to Fifty-seventh Street and walked east to the dealer's showroom. As she entered the shop, the smell was intoxicating. She had visited these rooms often as a child. Now, for a moment, she missed her father acutely, missed holding his hand, standing close to him and listening to the strange accents, shoptalk about past and current dealers in Europe and America, the price of instruments at auction, the values of particular violins, violas, violoncellos, who had restored or "butchered"—Fernand's word—which instrument in what shop. There would be laughter and gossip, talk of back cracks and sound post adjustment and the quality of repair. Mariana, listening, had learned.

The young receptionist, applying lipstick, looked up to say she was expected and could go directly to Baum's private office. He greeted her, dressed immaculately in a navy blazer.

"I've come to play the Swan one final time," she announced, not meeting his eyes.

He gazed at her with evident sympathy. She chose to say no more. He went back to the workshop and soon reappeared with the instrument in hand. "Come," he said, "there's an empty room for you." She followed him down the darkened passageway.

❧

In the tiny, soundproofed space, Mariana played the simple pieces Casals had taught her father, who in turn had taught her. Then she played Bach. After half an hour, she stopped, too unhappy to continue. She stroked the instrument's ribs and back, caressed the pegs, pressed her fingers to the silver ornamentation of the scroll and ran her lips along the smooth neck, remembering her last public performance with her father. They had played together at the Metropolitan Museum of Art in 2000 at a black-tie event for donors to the rare instruments collection.

When he accepted the invitation, Alexander had said, "You know, Mariana, this exposure will only increase the value of the Swan. To play it in the Mertens Gallery—with all those donors watching—raises its level yet another notch in the collector's eye. Though I myself don't care for such publicity, I must do this for you. Should you ever decide to part with it, you'll get an even higher price. I must secure your future."

Mariana sighed. "Don't do this for *me*, Papa. You've already done so much."

Alexander heard no irony in her answer. "You will, of course, join me there. I absolutely insist."

On that clear winter night, after the curator of the collection, Andrew Macintosh, introduced the evening, Alexander sat with his head bowed, Mariana beside him in a flowing silver gown. He stood and began to speak.

"Here is the magnificent Swan." Alexander removed the velvet drapery from the instrument and carried it forward. "It's still a mystery — one we may never solve — why *this* particular shape and *this* particular thickness of wood are calculated to produce such acoustical sonority. No experts have ever quite explained it and no one has ever improved on it. Let me play for you."

After, turning to Mariana, he had said, "Come, sweetheart, sit here next to me. Let's give our listeners the chance to compare. We shall play the first movement of the Bach D-Minor Suite, as I studied it with Casals."

He closed his eyes and waited for silence. When he lifted his bow, she lifted hers and, together, they played, in perfect unison of tone, fingering and bowing. When they came to the final note, Alexander rested his bow at his side and lowered his chin to his chest. Mariana, tears glistening on her cheeks, reached down to take his left hand. She raised it and kissed his fingers as the audience came to its feet.

❧

Mariana opened the door of the small, windowless room and went to return the instrument to Baum.

He invited her to sit. "Coffee?"

"Thank you, no."

Then, resuming the conversation he had started in the lobby at Tully Hall, Baum leaned across his desk and said, "What a disappointment for both of us that your father left the cello to this young man, Roselle. This is not what we envisioned, is it?"

Mariana shook her head.

"Alexander always told me he would leave the Swan to you,"

Baum continued. "And after you stopped playing, he particularly asked me to help by brokering a profitable sale. He trusted me and wanted me alone to handle the transaction. I, of course, had already begun the task of finding a buyer. In fact"—Baum leaned forward and lowered his voice—"I confide in you that I did make contact with a gentleman abroad who was interested in the whole collection—the Swan and all its copies—nothing less. This Roselle gift comes now as quite a surprise. My client will be disappointed, though I have not yet told him the deal is off." He paused, studying her face. "And you too must be very unhappy."

There was something in his manner Mariana did not trust. "My father spoke to me about it in advance," she lied. "There's nothing more to say. I understood his desire to place the instrument in the hands of a fine performer."

"And," Baum continued, "when he repaid the money I lent him to finance the purchase of the Swan, I offered to let him keep the funds and give me part ownership. He insisted he could not do this because the Swan would be yours one day, Mariana, and would give you financial security. He said he couldn't compromise that."

Mariana looked down and said nothing.

"The reward for my generosity, your father claimed, would come after his death, when I brokered the sale of the cello on your behalf."

"He paid you what he owed you," she said sharply. "And at the time, he had no idea I would no longer be playing. I understand his choice."

"Well, then, you've both made the right decision," Baum responded sourly. He was terse and she could see he did not believe her. "In Roselle, you've chosen well. Have you seen the *Times* review of the concert last night?"

He handed her the Arts section and Mariana read what she had to admit was a magnificent review. It made much of Claude's musical inheritance from her father and praised his sensitive interpretation of Brahms: "both impeccable and passionate, exultant and restrained." It called him a major—"arguably *the* major"—European talent on the instrument. And at the very end, it said, "To make up for the music world's loss of Alexander Feldmann, we are fortunate that Claude Roselle has donned his mentor's mantle on the concert stage." The Roselles would have a lot to celebrate, she thought with renewed resentment.

"A fine review. All one could hope for," Mariana said. "I enjoyed his performance. He's an exceptional cellist in the Feldmann tradition." She returned the newspaper to Baum and rose to leave. "I'll come back in a while, Hanns. We still have decisions to make about the copies." She was aware she was offering him nothing. The copies meant little without the great Swan.

"Stay a moment longer to refresh my memory. Let's see, there are nine copies here on my list. Let me ask Pierre to join us. He knows much more about the copies than I do, having worked on and adjusted them all so many times. I'll give him a ring."

Instants later, Pierre Fernand appeared in Baum's office. "'Ello, Mariana." He blew her a kiss. "I hear you have come to play the Swan. How do you find her?"

"Nonpareil, as ever."

"She needs a face-lift." He winked. "At a certain age, so do we all." Pierre assigned genders to the instruments he worked on—the Swan was female. "I sink she will be so much more beautiful when I have restored her."

"We are discussing the copies, Pierre. What can you tell us about them?"

"The copies, they are of different caliber, of course, though they are good enough instruments to play. Many young cellists would be happy with any one of them — particularly with the pedigree, the imprimatur of Feldmann. They have a certain value, after all, some of them better than others. I think none is better than your Vuillaume, Mariana, both to the eye and the ear, although of course this is a Frenchman speaking and a French opinion. Why don't you bring them here and we play them together and decide what is to be done? You surely don't intend to keep them all?"

"We would be happy to help you," Baum said.

"The copies are in my father's house in the Berkshires," she answered.

"Ah, such a beautiful place, Swann's Way." Fernand smiled. "I had pleasant visits there over the years. Have you been back since he died?"

"No. I haven't the heart to go back since I closed up the house in January. The memories are too raw." She paused. "And when will Claude Roselle take the cello back to Switzerland?"

"I have his promise he leaves it with me until I complete the restoration, as your father wished. It will take several months. Then he will return for it. But don't stay away, my dear. You, above all, will have to be the judge of my work. Young M. Roselle will have little basis to make the comparison. I shall always ask you to come and visit her as I work."

"Yes, we'll all be happy to have the Swan in America awhile longer. Don't hurry, Pierre," Baum said.

❧

On her way home, Mariana decided to walk past the apartment she had shared with Anton during the six years of their affair. The memories of those years both soothed and pained her. Soaring above Lincoln Center, the apartment, in a shining glass tower with views of the Hudson River, was on a dizzyingly high floor. It had a large living area and two small bedrooms that faced east and the rising sun. Anton had covered the walls, helter-skelter, with contemporary Russian paintings, and left the rest of the décor to Mariana. He did not care much about his surroundings, she learned, as long as they were comfortable and possessed of the finest sound systems. He listened to music constantly, sitting at the dining room table with a score in front of him, a pencil perched on his ear.

She and Anton had nested there whenever they shared time in New York. When he was away, she felt secure in his imagined presence. And when she was away on tour, she had only to conjure up the apartment to feel rooted.

Shortly after Mariana met him the first time, Pietovsky had had a heart attack. His doctors made him give up rich foods, tobacco, and alcohol. When, at twenty-five, Mariana met him again, he was slim and sober and had no recollection of their first meeting.

In their life together, Mariana watched over him with concern. "Have you taken your heart medicine yet?" she asked Anton one morning, emerging from their darkened bedroom into the blinding sunlight.

Anton leaned over the score of a Mendelssohn symphony, a cup of tea at his elbow. He was to conduct that night. Looking up, he beamed at her.

"Ah, at last, here is my beauty, my rising sun. No, I have not taken my medicine. I enjoy it more when you bring it to me and feed me each one."

"But what do you do when I'm not here or you're away from me?" she asked, laughing.

"I prefer to have heart attack and die!"

"Oh, for God's sake," she said, moving toward him. She fell into his embrace. With great tenderness, he kissed her and led her to the couch.

"Now, you sit here. I bring coffee. When you sleep so long, I miss talking to you."

"You talk to me anyway; you know, you talk in your sleep. All night."

"And what do I say?"

"Lento, allegro, con anima, andante—I don't know." Mariana smiled and patted his hand. "You're always conducting."

"I should say *appassionata*," he joked, "when I am lying with you. Now, sit here, I make coffee." A tea drinker, Anton had never properly learned to make coffee—grounds scattered all over the kitchen and also in her cup. The coffee was either brutally strong or watery, but she drank it gratefully in either case. Traveling with Mariana and living in hotels, Anton would call room service in the morning and, when the waiter appeared with breakfast on a rolling table, it would amuse him to ask Mariana, very formally, how she took her coffee, as if this had been their first night together and he hardly knew her. She would answer, "Oh, Maestro Pietovsky, please, with sugar and milk," and they would giggle after the waiter left the room.

Mariana stretched out on the couch and awaited her coffee. Anton returned with the morning's nasty brew and settled next to her. He lifted her legs across his lap, massaging her feet. "So, my treasure, my Fabergé egg, will you come tonight to my concert?"

"Of course," she answered. "I love you and I love Mendelssohn. How could it be better?"

"Could be better if we never left this apartment, we just stayed together here and made love and music."

"You're such a romantic," she answered, smiling, "but I quite agree. That would be a heavenly life."

"Ho, but the world would be deprived of your talent, Mariana. No more concerts. That would not be so good. Everyone would be angry with me. They would say, 'That old man, he stole the light from us. He stole the jewel, the beauty from our lives.'"

Mariana put her cup on the coffee table and, swinging her legs off his lap, wrapped her arms around his neck. She stared into his eyes and said gravely, "Anton, *you* are the jewel. You've made me understand how it feels to be loved and treasured, to be respected for my playing... *You* are the genius and I'm the lucky one... whatever happens."

"But what will happen, darling? What could ever happen?"

She drew back and studied his face but gave no answer. At twenty-seven, she had few illusions. She had not given up her own rent-controlled apartment; he had, after all, a wife.

❧

At seven forty-five, Mariana rushed into Cafe Luxembourg. She hadn't meant to keep Claude waiting but had been unable to find a taxi. That afternoon, she'd shaved her legs, washed, creamed, scented, and polished every inch of her body, then chose her clothes with care. She was radiant as she hurried into the restaurant, scanning the crowd at the noisy bar on the right. She did not see Claude, who would, at his height, have stood out. Anxiously, she looked around the room. *There* he was, sitting at a table in the far corner, chair turned so his legs could comfortably cross. He had a drink in one hand and his cell phone in the other. Seeing her, he snapped it shut and rose, as the waiter guided her to the table. She felt excited, too excited. He pulled out her chair, the one nearest his own, and she ordered gin on the rocks.

"I read the excellent review of your concert in the *Times* this afternoon. Congratulations. You must be thrilled and gratified."

"Yes, so much better that than a humiliation. Particularly if you want to impress a beautiful and knowledgeable woman." He smiled, his right cheek dimpling. "If the review were bad, then I would have had to sit here wondering if you would still come this evening!"

"Forgive me. There were no taxis."

The waiter brought her drink. Claude toasted her. "I'm very happy you came to hear me play, and on such short notice. I only wish I could return the favor. I have always heard you were the greatest talent of your generation."

Briefly, Mariana felt vexed. Was he suggesting that they, merely three years apart, were of different generations? She let it pass.

"And by giving up performing, you have cleared the way," Claude hastened to add, "for us lesser mortals to fight for your title."

Ah, she thought, he notices things. "Yes, it's interesting to see how legends grow, despite a lack of evidence. My reputation has only improved since I quit. It's amusing, but not something to take seriously!"

Claude took her hand. "I won't ask you why you stopped performing, since I don't yet know you well enough, but I hope to know you well enough very soon, and then I'll ask you to tell me. Your father must have been *désolé.* He was so proud of you."

She laughed. "Oh, yes, he moped and nagged. He claimed he was terribly disappointed in me and had wasted his time teaching me. But he was also competitive, you know? A very conflicted man."

Claude, puzzled, asked what she meant. Mariana said, "Let's not be serious tonight."

The waiter appeared and they ordered a second round of drinks, then appetizers: Mariana chose smoked salmon, and Claude, snails. Claude asked for the wine list. He moved his chair closer to hers so they could look at it together. "You're wearing a beautiful scent," he said, tucking back a straying wisp of her hair and dipping toward her neck. "You must tell me what it is so I can always bring it to you." He was flirting with her and she enjoyed it, but at that moment she remembered Anton. He had made the same promise.

They sipped their drinks and Claude asked, "Do you ever even touch the cello anymore?"

"Of course. Just this morning, I went to Baum & Fernand to play the Swan one last time."

Claude, surprised, said, "But I was there this afternoon! We could have gone together…"

"Did they tell you I had visited?"

He shook his head. "And why one *last* time, Mariana? You know I'll always share the instrument with you. We are now linked forever through the Swan. It would have been yours had you continued to play. That was always your father's intention, as I understand it."

"Perhaps." Her answer was cool. "In truth, I knew very

little of my father's intentions or, for that matter, of his life. He was a man of great charm, mystery, and contradictions."

Claude was thoughtful. "Maybe that's implicit in the nature of a great artist..."

"What?"

"The quality of mystery, privacy—a focus on one's art that makes one inaccessible."

"Maybe. Or possibly he was just a manipulative, selfish bastard who needed to control everything and everyone. Could that also be in the nature of a great artist?" She hoped this would shock him.

Claude's answer was self-deprecating. "Well, if that's the case, I shall always be at best a mediocre artist..."

As dinner progressed, Mariana grew warmer. They had much to talk about. She offered him a portion of her smoked salmon and he fed her snails, extracting them from their buttery shells, lifting them to her mouth. The waiter poured Pouilly-Fuissé. They discussed the Libbey dinner the previous night, the art collection, the ancient lady's amour propre, and the charms of Zena Padrova.

"It was very puzzling, you know," Claude confided. "My mother cried when she talked with Padrova at dinner. I've never seen her cry in public."

"Do you wonder what troubled her?"

"Yes, a little. But I'd never ask. I don't like to pry."

They continued talking about the music world, the careers of other cellists, what it was like to work with William Rossen, and Claude's immediate plans. In a week he was embarking on his first American concert tour, performing the Schumann concerto in six cities. Over a shared dish of bouillabaisse, she asked about his parents' relationship.

"It seems to me really more a working friendship than a marriage, but they are very close, as friends, I mean." He stared at Mariana intently. "This lack of passion would not satisfy me, but they seem to enjoy their independence."

"How very Swiss," she said, and realized she might have insulted him. Of course *he* did not know about his mother's "intense and passionate" love affair with Alexander. Her own knowledge, acquired so recently and shockingly, was a card best kept in her deck.

Claude poured more wine. "I realize this is a delicate subject, but I want to tell you I'm aware of what you and your mother sacrificed so that your father could purchase the Swan. He often talked about the enormous expense, and how for many years your resources went largely to paying off the cost of the instrument. The Swan was a member of your family."

"We did not suffer," she lied.

"Do you now feel very upset with him?" He took her hand. "Or with me?"

Her answer was dismissive. "Don't let that trouble you. Why would I be angry with *you*? Although it came as a surprise, as you noticed in Boston, I understood I could lose the Swan. My father was never very good at keeping his promises."

"This was not my impression."

"At least he left it to you and not to one of his mistresses." Feeling the imminence of tears, she tried to sound nonchalant. Claude raised an eyebrow but did not probe further.

After a long silence, she continued, "I do have one favor to ask. I would prefer that people think my father and I made the decision *together* to give you the cello. That he consulted me."

"Of course, but may I ask why?"

"Because it would be tiresome to have people constantly asking how I feel about my father's decision. If they think I made the decision with him, they'll be satisfied."

"I assure you, then, that's what I will say. And I will tell my mother never to discuss it with anyone. I'll forbid her to." He lifted his hand to stroke her cheek. "I know it's bold to ask you so many questions so soon, but I'm eager to know you, and to know you very well. If you won't yet tell me why you stopped performing in public, will you tell me if you were very much in love with Pietovsky?"

Mariana was taken aback. She paused and looked into his eyes. "Yes, yes I was," she answered. "Very much."

"Ah." He sighed. "So difficult. I myself have never been very much in love. Not yet. Was it terrible when his wife—"

"Enough talk," Mariana said abruptly.

"I quite agree. Enough, at least for tonight. We have come a certain distance to knowing each other. Now to something more pleasurable even than talking with you."

"Yes," she said, looking at her watch. "I must get home and you must get some sleep."

She pushed back her chair. Impulsively, he leaned down to kiss her, putting his arms around her neck and pulling her toward him. She did not want to resist. "I don't need sleep, Mariana. I know what I need. We must gather up our things and go back to my hotel." He kissed her again, lingering. "Must I wait to pay the bill or shall we make a dash for it?"

"Pay quickly, please."

Roselle waved for the waiter and the check.

CHAPTER SIX

Claude

"How was your evening, darling?" Francine was packing for her return to Lugano, her large suitcase open on the bed. In her pink dressing gown, wearing no makeup, Claude thought she looked much older.

"Very pleasant," he said, settling into a wing chair by the window. He cast a leg over the side. "We ate at Cafe Luxembourg. I must say the food was marvelous." He looked out at Park Avenue. "It was Mariana's suggestion."

Folding her evening dress, Francine paused to study him. "You had dinner with Mariana? I hadn't realized she'd invited you..."

"No, Maman, it was I who invited her." He opened the *New York Times*. "Had it been the reverse, she would of course have invited *you* also."

The hotel room was furnished in mahogany and chintz. It strove for Old World elegance and, to a degree, attained it. "I'm not so sure," said Francine.

"Will Papa be home when you return?"

"Are you changing the subject?"

He smiled at her. "I am."

She packed a stack of blouses: pastel pink, white, blue, and lemon yellow silk. "Yes. He finishes in Zurich and arrives just as I do, so we'll have time together before he goes again to Vienna."

"That's nice. You've seen so little of each other these past months." Claude turned a page. "And what did *you* do last night?"

"I had dinner with the Kappelmans, old friends of Alexander's."

"Then they must be very old," he teased. She glared at him.

"They were his colleagues at Juilliard. Far younger than he—as, in the end, was everyone. The death of his friends disturbed and saddened Alexander very much—to see his generation pass away..."

"I can imagine," Claude said, his leg jittering over the chair arm.

"I'm not at all certain you can."

"Come, Maman, finish packing and get dressed. Then we'll have breakfast. You need some nourishment; you seem a little grumpy. I'll just sit here and finish the paper, so I don't distract you."

❦

At Le Pain Quotidien on Lexington Avenue, they took a table for two in the rear. Once the waiter had taken their order, Francine asked, "And what did she have to say for herself? Did you learn anything interesting?"

"I'm sorry, who?"

"Mariana. Mariana Feldmann."

"She's very charming. We had a lovely time."

"Oh?"

Claude spoke carefully. "She's the daughter of my great teacher and your beloved friend. Poor Mariana has lost her mother, her father, and now the Swan. I think we owe her some consideration. She was upset, we could see, by her father's decision to leave the cello to me.

"There's one more thing, Maman. I promised Mariana that neither you nor I would mention that this decision came as a surprise to her. We are to make it clear, instead, that this was a decision she participated in and sanctioned. It means a great deal to her." He studied Francine's face. "It will keep people from asking unpleasant questions. I hope you understand."

"I really can't see what difference it makes. Does she want to be known as your generous benefactor? It was Alexander's gift, not hers—"

Claude interrupted her, his voice stern. "I made her this promise. Both you and I must keep it. There is nothing to discuss."

They walked in silence back to the hotel and, as they parted, Claude bent down to kiss her. "Have a good flight; all my best to Papa. I'll be home in a few weeks."

❧

Hurrying from the taxi the night before and rushing down the corridor to his hotel room, he and Mariana had flung themselves across the bed. She had wrapped her legs around him, pulling him against her, greedy and urgent, perhaps a little drunk. But so was he. Her black hair splayed over the bed. They undressed each other with haste and made love for much of the night. Briefly, at two o'clock, he slept. When he woke, she was stroking him so lightly his flesh prickled. Then she straddled him, staring down from her dark height with an inward-facing half-veiled gaze. She asked him what he wanted from her. Whatever he wanted, she said, was what she wanted too.

"To spend this week in bed with you," he answered.

In the morning, Mariana took a rapid shower and brewed a cup of coffee from the room's two-cup electric pot, then dressed herself once more in the previous evening's finery. When she was a college student, she told Claude, this was called "the walk of shame."

"I don't understand."

"You know. When your clothing makes it clear you've slept in someone else's bed."

He laughed. "You mean, gold sandals and a beaded bag are not the usual morning wear in Manhattan?"

"Here, perhaps, but I was a student in Indiana."

"My mother leaves this afternoon," said Claude. "Her flight's at three o'clock, I think. I'll spend the morning with her and when she leaves for the airport, I'll call you, if that would be all right with you."

He hoped she wouldn't run into Francine in the hotel lobby. His mother would be distressed and disapproving. It would be such a bore to have to calm and reassure her before her flight departed.

She stroked his bare chest, letting her hand drop to his thigh. "See you tonight, then?"

"Certainly tonight."

"Shall we try another restaurant," she asked, "or do you want more of the same?"

"Much more of the same."

❦

Once Francine left, Claude moved to a less expensive hotel on the West Side, the Beacon, on Broadway and within walking distance of Mariana's apartment. Trees were thickening into leaf and early spring flowers bloomed in the park. At his invitation, Mariana stayed with him. They made short forays to museums, to Central Park, and to Zabar's up the street. They ate out or brought picnics of fruit, pâté, cheese, and wine to the hotel, and Claude brought her roses each day. In bed, they made love and talked.

"Were you very fond of my father?" she asked one morning.

"He was always special to me. But to be honest — until I was old enough to understand how great a musician and teacher he was, how lucky I was to study with him — I mostly looked forward to his visits because he arrived with chocolate éclairs. Little éclairs from the bakery in Montagnola — in a white box with string he let me untie."

"How sweet!" She was sarcastic. Claude seemed not to notice.

"And I liked him because he made my mother happy. Funny that a child would know that, but she did seem so different when he visited — gayer, lighter, more lenient with me. They laughed a lot together," Claude continued, "much more than she did with my father. My mother liked to have fun, to go out. I often imagined, when she and your father left our house in the evening, they were about to go dancing in some cabaret. Your father dressed with so much style. He had such worldly elegance — to me, he looked like a movie star. Did you feel the same way?"

"Oh, I did. He had that effect on everyone, it seemed. He was all charm, handsome and debonair. Yet he was a boy from Albany."

"What's Albany? I don't know it. What does it mean to be from Albany?"

She ran her fingers through his curls. "Only that he wasn't

exposed to much besides music as a kid. His parents were shop owners, immigrants, Jews from Vienna. They loved music and gave the children lessons, but they didn't envision a life in music for their son. His father hated the idea. He wanted his children to have secure, middle-class professions. So Alexander had to break away. At sixteen, he went by himself to New York. The rest you know..."

"Yes," he answered, enfolding her hand in his own. "Of course, as a little boy I heard so much about you from your father. I knew, for example, that this mysterious girl named Mariana played the cello well, extremely well, better than I could hope to."

She propped herself up on her elbow. "And *your* father?"

"What about my father?"

"Did he like Alexander? Were they friends?"

"They were very cordial. I don't remember that he was much around when your father came. But I don't think they were unfriendly. My father too was busy, conducting all over Europe, and he was usually away when your father arrived. My mother, at those times, would stay home so I could have my lessons. I think M. Feldmann was always more my *mother's* friend."

Mariana sighed. "I think you're right."

⁂

The Do Not Disturb sign remained on the door. Preparing for his concert tour, keeping his hands in shape, Claude put his mute on the cello and played. He practiced Kodály and Bach and, of course, the Schumann concerto. Mariana—holding a cup of coffee—lay naked on the bed, listening intently and critiquing his technique. Claude recognized her father's teaching in what she said and how she said it. Feldmann's presence in the room was almost palpable.

"Don't rush through that passage. You need to vary the tempo, make each return to the refrain slightly different. You can't be lazy, not for a second."

He tried again.

"You mustn't always emphasize the beginning of the phrase," she'd say. "And don't play repeated phrases in the same way. Use your imagination. Speak to me in the language of the music." If a passage were just right, "Bravo," she'd call out. "*Yes!*"

They turned their cell phones off. When he left to buy flowers or wine, however, Claude would call Sophie and leave messages, hoping she would not answer. There were several messages from Francine, home in Lugano. Finally, he called her back. He told her he couldn't stay long on the phone.

"What's the great rush?" his mother asked. "It's eight thirty in the morning in New York, if I am not mistaken."

"I'm practicing, Maman, I'm always practicing this week. You know I must prepare for this tour."

"All right. I won't disturb you," she said resentfully.

"Thank you."

Outside, on the city pavement, Claude felt unmoored. He hurried back to the hotel. Never before had he experienced this sense that someone important was absent when he was alone. It was unnerving.

The moment came, each morning, when he put the instrument away and joined Mariana in bed. She held out her arms to him and joked that she'd fallen under his spell in the course of three Brahms sonatas on that first night in Tully Hall, that his music, not him, caused her feverish, uncontrollable desire.

"Why try to control desire?" he asked.

"Fires are always dangerous, Claude, there are reasons to extinguish them. But do I look like I'm trying?"

"Not very hard." He kissed her. "And neither am I. There will be nothing left of me when I start this tour but a cello and an empty suit."

From time to time he could hear a television and the sound of news or the canned laughter of a situation comedy in another room. The chambermaids rolled carts along the hall. But for him, there was only Mariana, always her lush nakedness, the sex, the stories of her father, the music. For now, he wanted nothing more.

She withheld some part of herself. Although he tried all week to learn more about her past, she would deflect his questions. And when he mentioned the Swan, she would cover his mouth with her hand and say, "No, let's not spoil anything. For now, let's live only in the present."

This was fine with him. But as their week together drew to its end, she withdrew. This trip, he told himself, had brought him luck—the success of his debut at Tully Hall, the fling with the lithe beauty beside him, the resplendent cello. He wanted her to feel as happy as he did, although he could see she did not.

As they returned to the hotel from a long walk in Central Park, she suddenly asked him if he had "someone" in Switzerland—a girlfriend there?

Caught off guard, he joked. "At our age, I think we should call them lovers."

She made him stop walking and look at her directly. "You know what I'm asking, Claude. Call it what you will: a lover, a mistress, a serious relationship, a partner, a girlfriend. You know what I mean. You are thirty-five years old. Surely there's someone in your life. Tell me."

He put his hands on her shoulders. "Mariana, I have had

only casual relationships without commitments. I have little time for anything serious. My life is the cello and the cello is a stern mistress. It is so hard to launch a career." Claude frowned. "No one knows better than you how consuming this is and how little it leaves you for the rest of life. I don't want to make anyone unhappy; I don't want to feel guilty. I don't want to be a bad husband or, worse yet, an absent father. No, there's no one in Switzerland, or anywhere else, whom I would call a partner in my life." He paused, then asked, "And you?"

Staring straight into his eyes, she answered, "Not since Anton." She dropped her head to his chest. "Our lives, yours and mine, have so little way to connect, Claude."

He stroked her hair. "Our lives are forever connected—through the Swan and your father and the way we care for each other."

He wondered if this were true. They walked back to the hotel. In their room, he took off his jacket and shoes and began to undress her. He saw something in her manner that he had not seen before—something profoundly sad. He took off his watch, his shirt and pants. The bed had been remade by the chambermaid while they were out. There were chocolates on the pillow. He brushed these aside and lowered her to the smooth, cool sheets. She brought her arms across her body to support her breasts. Claude reached over and spread her arms wide, then tenderly touched her wet cheeks. He knelt on the carpet at her feet, kissing her instep and toes. "Mariana, your legs are so long; I will start here, slowly. It will be hours before I reach your calves, your knees, and every place beyond. Have you the time? Will you open yourself to me?"

"I have time," she answered, her breathing shallow. "It's you who has to go."

"I'll make time for *this* journey. No shortcuts," he whispered. He licked her feet, then ankles, hearing the rapid intake of breath and then her soft sharp groan.

❧

When he left for the West Coast, he said he'd try to call every day. He was playing in Los Angeles, Seattle, Portland, Denver, Houston, and finally, Baltimore. When he finished, he planned to return directly to Lugano from Baltimore, where his final concert was scheduled, two weeks hence.

"I miss you already," she said.

Claude, preparing for departure, reminded Mariana that he would return the moment Pierre Fernand summoned him. As soon as the Swan was restored and ready to be played in public, they would meet again. And if that turned out to be too long to wait, they could plan a vacation together. They could meet in Europe, if she wished to "cross the pond."

Pleased with himself for remembering that expression, he repeated it. Yet nothing he said could make her smile. "My dear Mariana," he finally said, "you've been left too often by a cellist."

Hailing a cab, he loaded his suitcase and his cello into the trunk and they kissed goodbye. As the taxi pulled from the curb, he saw her sling her bag across her shoulder and, he assumed, head home toward the apartment to which he'd not yet been invited.

❧

In the Sky Club at Kennedy Airport, the wine was second-rate *vin ordinaire*, but he drank it anyway, hoping to sleep on the plane. He was relieved to be alone. Although he had no desire to, he called Sophie. Days had gone by since he had spoken to her. The connection was good.

"Tell me all your news first," he said. "I insist."

She informed him about the museum retreat, the plans they were developing for an exhibition of the collection's Spanish holdings and the Velázquez they were hoping to authenticate, a painting she particularly loved. He could tell she was trying not to sound reproachful.

"I know your trip has been very eventful," she concluded.

"Yes, this has been an exhilarating time."

"Your mother told me about the gift of the great cello."

Annoyed with Francine, he continued, "I've met influential people in the music world. I've been practicing each morning and, of course, I've visited Pierre Fernand every afternoon."

"The luthier?"

"Yes, the man who will restore the Silver Swan."

"I'm very happy for you, Claude," Sophie said. "Your mother and I had lunch together two days ago. She invited me to celebrate your good fortune. We toasted you."

Claude said nothing. He took a sip of wine and looked around the club. A family played cards at the next table. An elderly couple slept, snoring lightly. A woman brushed her hair.

"Are you there?"

"They've called my flight. I'll have to board soon."

"And was Feldmann's daughter nice? Your mother said you both met her."

"Her name is Mariana, and as far as I can tell she's quite a lovely person. She used to be an important cellist, but she no longer plays as a soloist."

"Yes, so I heard," said Sophie. "It was generous of her and, of course, her father to leave you this great instrument. It must be difficult to know how properly to thank her."

Ah, he thought, Maman is doing what I asked her to, including Mariana in the gift. He replied, "Indeed, I must give that some serious thought. A proper gift."

"Perhaps I can help you to think of the right thing."

"That would be lovely, Sophie. Do try to think of something. And now I have to go. I'll call you as often as possible. Goodbye for now."

"*Ciao*, darling. Come home as soon as you can. I've something wonderfully interesting to tell you."

"Why not tell me now?"

"No, it must wait until we are together."

He boarded as soon as first class was announced. Thinking of the Silver Swan, he strapped his Tecchler into the seat beside him. The flight attendant took his coat and he accepted the offer of another glass of wine. It would surely put him to sleep. He kicked off his shoes and, sinking into the leather seat, thought of Mariana, the smell of her still on his clothes. Perhaps he would miss her.

The man behind him leaned forward. "Did you buy a ticket for that thing?"

"Excuse me?"

"I mean, did you have to pay for it? My Lord, what an expense."

Claude turned around to answer. "Yes, I buy a ticket for my cello every time I fly. Traveling with a cello is like traveling with a woman—complicated, expensive, and cumbersome. But there are two positives..."

"Yes?"

"I eat its food, and the instrument doesn't talk."

The man laughed at Alexander's old joke. Claude settled back in his seat.

CHAPTER SEVEN

Mariana

One week after Claude left New York, Mariana, at Heinrich Baum's urging, decided to travel to Stockbridge to check on the house and make sure the copies of the Swan were safely stored. Baum had asked her to locate their ownership papers in the event she decided to sell. When Alexander died, she had departed Swann's Way in haste, leaving behind disorder. She'd not been back for months.

Claude had called twice, from Los Angeles and then from Portland. He proudly read her his stellar reviews. He had launched his American career. The calls were brief. He asked very little about how she was spending her time but regaled her with stories of his travels. "America is vast and dull and provincial for the most part," he joked, "but it does have some beautiful concert halls. And a few beautiful women, you being the foremost example."

She told him she would soon be going to Swann's Way.

He seemed disconcerted. "Why will you go?"

"I have to put the estate in order. The house needs work. There are boxes of CDs and cartons of old vinyl recordings. There are nine copies of the Swan and God knows how many music stands and metronomes and old bows with stiff horsehair, gifts and trophies and framed covers of albums and honorary degrees. Stuff, lots of stuff. You are lucky you haven't faced this yet, Claude. My father's career spanned three-quarters of a century and he saved absolutely everything."

"How long will you stay?" He paused. "And will you go alone?"

"Yes, I'll go alone and stay until I'm too sad and too resentful to bear it any longer. You know, one of my friends suggested I just throw everything into a dumpster. She said I'd done enough for him."

Claude was shocked. "But of course you couldn't do that, could you?"

"I'm rather tired of making my father my life's work," she answered dryly, "but no, no I couldn't."

"I'm sure the papers and scores, all these things will be valuable. Some library will want them." He was silent for a while. "Perhaps I could join you there for a few days."

"I thought you had to rush back to Switzerland."

"I have a little time to visit you, but only if I have the discipline to prepare for my next concerts while I'm there. You must force me to work. In any case, I've always wanted to see Swann's Way. Your father spoke of it very often."

Mariana felt a rush of joy. "I'll wait to go up there until you're finished with the tour. And I'll whip you if you don't practice."

"I wish you would."

They agreed he would come after his last performance in Baltimore and she would pick him up at the Albany airport. "Ah, Albany," he said.

⁂

Mariana drove to Stockbridge on a bright, spring morning. It was easier to return to Swann's Way, high on a mountainside and far from town, knowing Claude would join her. She'd always been nervous about staying in this remote place alone. As she parked her car next to Alexander's old Cadillac and let herself into the house, she felt a wave of fear and grief. She brought her cello and suitcase into the foyer and wandered through the house, studying each room from its doorway, the photographs and paintings and mountain views, as if there were a velvet rope preventing her from entering.

That afternoon, she met Claude at the airport. They embraced and hurried to the car. As they drove through Albany, past the huge towers of the state office buildings, Claude asked, "Now where exactly was your father born?" When Mariana said she had no idea, he was silent.

She said, "This is not a pilgrimage, darling."

They crossed the Hudson River, and city gave way to countryside. Claude admired the picturesque white frame houses, churches, low stone walls, open fields rising to the base of green mountains. Mount Greylock appeared in the distance. The town of Williamstown, he said, was nearly as well tended as a Swiss village.

Turning south on Route 7, she asked, "How long can you stay?"

"I'm not sure—about a week, not more."

He put his hand on her leg and stroked it. They were quiet for a while, passing through the Berkshire towns. Noticing the sign for Tanglewood, Claude asked if they could visit. "Did you ever play there?"

"Sure," she answered. She wished they were already at Swann's Way so she could press her body against his and puncture the fragile membrane that seemed to separate them after two weeks apart. "I played in the student orchestra for years, I played chamber music, and I took lessons every summer, at first with my father's students. Later, as you know, I went to study with János Starker at Indiana University."

"Oh, yes, Starker. How did your father react when you decided to become a Starker student? It seems to me they had very little in common musically."

"My father acted morose and petulant, but proud that I'd been accepted to Starker's class." She paused. "So often he was like that — impressed but resentful, almost competitive, all at the same time. I found it hard to know how to succeed, how to please him. He would reinforce my belief in my own talent, only to chip away at it."

She focused on the road ahead. "When I was young, he expected me to attend his master classes, but if I spoke up, even just to express an opinion I'd heard him expound one thousand times, he would contradict me harshly in that public setting to humiliate me, never mind that I was only repeating his own idea. I was not to steal one watt from his limelight. And yet he pushed me to achieve, to become famous, but only as the inheritor of his own talent."

"Which you certainly are known to be," Claude said gently. "But then you stopped playing."

"I'd been traveling a great deal, giving recitals and playing with orchestras. Finally, in 2002, I was deemed important enough to make my first solo appearance here with the Boston Symphony to play the Saint-Saëns concerto. But six months before the concert, I had to cancel. As you can imagine, that put a dent in my popularity."

"I can imagine," he said.

"I really had no choice, even though no one believed it." She paused. "My father certainly didn't."

"What happened?"

"I don't want to talk about it. Not just yet."

⁂

Although she would not tell Claude about it, Mariana remembered all too vividly the beginning of the end of her solo career. In late 2001 she had arrived in Frankfurt for a performance of the Elgar concerto with the Frankfurt Radio Symphony Orchestra. Anton would conduct, and they were to go from there to Italy for a brief vacation before he went to visit his wife in Moscow. These visits, Mariana had—for lack of choice—come to accept.

In her dressing room on the night of the concert, she had just slipped into a shimmering gown when there was a tap on the door. She turned and saw Zena Padrova peeking in, her pale blue eyes twinkling.

"I may come in, dahling? Before the concert?" She was already entering the small room, her plump body clad in an elegant dark red dress, her jewels immensely bright at ears and throat. She carried her long mink coat, which she dropped on a chair by the door.

"Of course."

"I come to have a moment with you by myself, but I won't stay long. I remember one wants to prepare in the head." She smacked her own head, smiling. "Here"—she moved toward Mariana—"I help you to close your gown in back."

"How wonderful to see you, Zena. What brings you to Frankfurt?" Mariana was again facing the mirror. She tried to hunch down so the much shorter woman could reach the fasteners. Mme Padrova looked around the small room. "I should get the chair, Marushka, to reach you. You know," she confided, "I never wore underwear when I played concerts." Mariana looked surprised. "It was so much more comfortable, and under so many layers of fabric in those big gowns, who would be able to find anything of interest?"

"But didn't it tickle?"

"Oh, yes. But nicely." She smiled mischievously and Mariana laughed, tossing back her head. Her long, curling hair slipped back over her shoulders. Finished with her task, Mme Padrova stood back and admired the bronze silk gown, which glowed even here in the dull light of the dressing room.

"You know, my dear," Mme Padrova continued, "long ago when I used to go to Bergdorf to try on concert gowns, I would ask for a chair to put in front of the three-way mirrors. Then, once I had on the gown, I would sit down and put apart my knees as wide as I could to make sure the cello would fit between. One time there was a new sales consultant who watched me do this. She said, 'Madame,' very indignantly, 'we don't allow such clientele here at Bergdorf Goodman,' and ran away to find her manager." Mme Padrova roared with laughter and plucked at Mariana's arm. "You can imagine how angry was the manager when she came and saw it was me. 'You stupid woman,' she said to the shopgirl, 'this is great Russian cellist Mme Zena Padrova. Do you even know what is a cello?' The poor young thing burst into tears. It was so funny. This I always remember."

Mariana smiled and looked anxiously at the clock on the wall. Through the filthy yellowed glass, she could see that the time of her performance was approaching and she could hear the loud applause for Anton and the orchestra as he finished the opening piece. Next it would be her turn. She faced the mirror to brush her hair and apply the lipstick and dark mascara one must never put on before the gown.

Mme Padrova reached down for her coat and moved toward the door. "I go now, Mariana, and come back after. You look like goddess. Your father would be so impressed if he could be here to listen. Break a leg, dahling. We talk later."

The door burst open and Anton, in concert tails, mopping his brow with an ironed handkerchief, hurried in past Mme Padrova, giving her a nod. He offered Mariana his arm. She picked up her Vuillaume and the bow, navigating through the narrow door as her guest made way for her. Minutes later, the conductor swept her onto the stage, stepping back as the crowd rose to welcome her with a standing ovation. The orchestra members tapped their bows on the music stands and stamped their feet.

Mariana blinked at the bright stage lights and smiled, bowing only slightly to keep her gown in place. In her high heels, she made her way toward her chair on a raised platform just below Anton's, stopping to shake the concertmaster's hand and to receive a reassuring kiss on her own hand from Anton, now on the podium and barely taller than she. After the audience quieted, she looked up at Anton, raised her bow high, and attacked the opening solo phrase of the Elgar concerto.

Alexander had had a student, a charming fellow named Stefan, from Poland, who could entertain people by imitating the performance styles of all the great cellists. He was an astute mimic. Alexander often asked him to entertain the other students during master classes. "There is a lesson in this," Alexander told Mariana, in private. "You see how silly one can look onstage if one doesn't master one's gestures. All that smiling to oneself and frowning and furrowing and humming and flinging about of the arms, it's distracting and undignified. And," he continued, "in case you think Stefan doesn't imitate me out of fear, I assure you this is not the case. It's because I am a bad subject, as you should be also. One must keep facial expressions and mannerisms to a minimum and give such clowns no material to work with. One must play with restraint so the audience can focus on the music." Mariana had learned this lesson well.

Onstage that night, she played with no histrionics, despite her fierce concentration. With only an occasional nod to Anton, and with eyes mostly closed, she used the strength of her muscled arms and back to extract a powerful sound from the Vuillaume. Her performance was masterful, nuanced and sensitive. When she finished, satisfied with her playing, she flashed her broad grin at the audience, bowing in all directions as they stood to applaud. Anton stepped down to embrace her.

The audience shouted and whistled. This was the prize, the gold ring captured. To receive this gratitude and appreciation was thrilling. But recently she had felt herself losing confidence that she would arrive at this moment without mishap. The more widely she traveled, the more important the concerts she was invited to play, the more fearful she became, unless she were with Anton, whom she trusted and whose mere presence with her onstage restored her nerve.

In the beginning, their affair had been the subject of endless gossip. Now, after five years, no one but her father cared. He seemed to feel excluded from his old friendship with Anton and jealous of Mariana's admiration for him. He also resented how obviously she had replaced him on Anton's concert stage. About this, she felt guilty, but her father was now eighty-one years old. He had had his great career.

After the Elgar and the many returns to the stage demanded by her audience, she and Anton retired to their respective dressing rooms for the intermission. She was finished. He had ahead of him the Brahms Symphony No. 3 in F Major. She poured herself a tall glass of iced water and unfastened her dress, though she did not remove it. Then she settled in her chair and closed her eyes to relive the performance. As the music began again onstage, she heard another tap on the door and Mme Padrova appeared again. "May I?" she asked. Mariana gestured an invitation. In the warmest terms, she congratulated Mariana on her superlative performance. Then she drew up a chair and faced Mariana, knees to knees. Taking her hands, the elderly woman looked up into Mariana's face. "I come to tell you something, my dear, that you may or may not yet know, but yet you must know it, and though you may think it is not my business, I have always loved you since you were a very little girl and I still do. You are my best friend's daughter."

Mariana smiled warmly. "Yes, I know. And I feel close to you."

"I have heard through endless Russian grapevine that Anton will finally bring his wife to America. He has taken apartment in New York for her and him. And I also have heard that she has made him promise to give up love affair with you."

Mariana blanched. "He has said nothing of this to me, Zena. Why would he not tell me, if it were true?"

Madame Padrova shed small tears of sympathy. "Because, like most men, he is coward when it comes to such things. And because he loves you. This he says always. But he has been married many years and also he loves his wife. She is older than you, though not as old as he. And he loves his daughters and their babies. He will not leave her."

"I see," Mariana said quietly. "If it's true, I should thank you for telling me."

"Is true." She paused. "Do you want to talk, Marushka?"

"No. Not now. Not yet." She looked up. "Have you told my father?"

"Of course not. It is for you to know first." Mme Padrova gathered up her things and, kissing her, left Mariana in the dim room.

That evening after the concert, she and the conductor attended the reception. Back at their hotel room, they packed. They were to spend the next three days together in Italy, taking a late-night flight to Milan. Mariana folded the bronze gown into her suitcase and changed into jeans. She was quiet while Anton prattled on about the Brahms, which she, lost in thought in her dressing room, had not heard. They taxied to the airport and went to the executive lounge. Anton stashed their bags in the luggage closet at the entrance, and Mariana, carrying her cello, went to find a place to settle. She heard Anton's hearty laugh and looked back to see him chatting with someone she didn't know. The man held a violin case. When Anton joined her, he sank into a chair and smiled at her.

"You know, feels like living room in these airport clubs. Is where I most often see old friends these days — other musicians coming and going, everybody traveling. Just last week I met, in airport in Zurich, the conductor Bernard Roselle with his son, Claude—a promising cellist but not so good as my Marushka. These clubs are like little salons, little chamber music halls. Here we should play concerts." He looked around, then laughed. "Ah, of course, no pianos."

"I hope you won't meet anyone else tonight," she said as she rose to bring him tea and mix a packet of hot chocolate for herself. She placed his cup on the table between their chairs, brushing off crumbs. Then she sat beside him.

"Anton, Zena Padrova came to tell me you will be bringing your wife to America soon. Is it true?"

He looked at her sadly and lowered his balding head. He was shaking, and when he looked up again, he appeared stricken. "Yes, my pet, my Marushka, it is so. She should not have told you. I planned to tell you in Italy."

Mariana believed him.

"Olga long has wanted to come. Her career no longer keeps her in Moscow. It is largely over. And though the children and grandchildren will stay, she is ready to be with me and travel to visit with them. You know, I am getting old and she is not so much younger. It is time we take care of each other. And you, you are so young. Is not right for you to take care of another old man."

"Is she very angry with you about me?"

"She will forgive me if it is over, really over. We've been married for many years, more than forty years. I think she knows how I love you. She chose to stay in Moscow when I came to America. She will recover."

"Will I?" She began to cry, awaiting his answer. He nodded his head slowly. "Yes, my pet, you will. You are young.

You have everything — beauty and talent and passion. You are a special woman, Marushka; you will be loved. Very much loved."

"Anton, you have given me courage, belief in myself. How will I have it without you?"

"You will find it, and it will be your own," he answered. "And you will have me always in your heart and I will have you in mine."

She pressed his hand to her heart. He looked suddenly amused. "And think how happy this will make your father!"

They sat together quietly until they boarded the plane to Milan.

❧

Passing Tanglewood, Claude opened the passenger window to breathe in the mountain air. "Have you been forgiven for canceling your concert?"

"Oh, yes. It was so many years ago. And after a while, the talk and speculation died down and people seemed to forget I'd ever been asked to play. They stopped asking if I would perform again."

They drove down the main street of Stockbridge and, two miles west of town, turned left toward Swann's Way. In the lengthening afternoon shadows, light filtered through the woods. The trees, leafing out weeks later here than in Central Park, wore a pale, lacy green. They entered the long, unpaved driveway and began the steep ascent.

The house stood, its four brick chimneys raised like outstretched arms, in a high clearing, atop a large expanse of rolling, rising lawn. The long path from garage to house was bordered by stone walls and stately maples. Dappled light flashed off the patterned slate roof. "Come into Feldmann's palace," she said, leading Claude to the door, "where celestial music is made."

She walked him through the rooms. He wanted to examine everything—each chair, each bed, each bookshelf—but she said there would be time for all that. He picked up a photograph of her as a child; in it she looked fragile. Then he looked at a photograph of Pilar and whistled. "What a beauty!"

"Yes, she was. She once was."

"Did you have great times with your father when you were young? When he came to Lugano, he was always so much fun. He liked to make me laugh. But only when we weren't working."

Mariana was thoughtful before answering. "When I was a kid, I loved it when he came home. Life got so much more interesting. Sometimes, on Saturdays or school vacations, I would get dressed nicely and he would take me around with him to the luthier shops, orchestra rehearsals, or lunch in fancy restaurants, or even to the tailor who made his clothes. I thought he was very handsome and everyone we met seemed so pleased to see him. I felt very important to be with him."

"I can imagine," Claude said.

"But he wasn't home very often, and even when he was, he didn't have much time for me."

As the sun dipped toward the western mountains, Mariana took Claude to her father's studio, where she removed the copies of the Silver Swan from the safe Alexander had installed. For insurance purposes, and in order to protect the instruments from fire, flood, or theft, he had built a steel room within the room. She removed two oil paintings and slid open the false wall panel behind them. The heavy door behind the panel bore a combination lock—its code the date of his debut recital and her birthday. She opened it. Inside, in a climate-controlled vault, eight copies of the famous Strad hung on velvet straps. The Stradivarius was of course in New York with Baum & Fernand, but these mute versions—lined up like soldiers, as if they waited for someone to say "at ease"—were still hers.

Claude sat on a chair in the living room. One by one she pulled the celli down and brought them to him, crossing and recrossing the large entrance hall. She placed the copies, as well as the Vuillaume she'd brought with her, in a circle—their scrolls resting on couches and chairs, their end pins pointing in. One by one she tuned them as Claude watched. She would ask him to play each one for her.

Surveying the circle of touching pins, she suddenly remembered a dinner she and her father had been invited to in Stockbridge. She told Claude the story.

"After a Tanglewood concert, we drove together to this vast house, on Main Street, where the Turnbulls, our hosts, live. They're a very old New England family—quite pleased with themselves. Our host wore a velvet smoking jacket and dainty satin slippers, which my father much admired. Mrs. Turnbull served roast lamb and sweet potato soufflé, and, for dessert, something called a ginger fool, which she proudly explained was an early American confection her family had prepared for hundreds of years.

"I really can't remember why, but Richardson Turnbull started talking about the family plot in the nearby Stockbridge cemetery. The Turnbulls, he announced with pride, were buried in a large circle with toes all pointing inward, kind of like these cello pins. This way, he said, on Judgment Day, when they arose, they would see only each other, all Turnbulls, a circle of only those deserving enough to look at each other for eternity and share their ascent. He said there was still room for him and for his wife, though their children would have to begin a new circle. Unfortunately, my father and I laughed and laughed, assuming he was joking. We were very embarrassed when we realized he was serious. 'How very original,' my father had managed to say."

"You Americans," Claude said, smiling. He rose from the couch. "You make so much of this brief history of yours." Pointing to the circle of celli, he said, "This is for tomorrow." He took Mariana's hand and led her back up the stairs to the room where she'd told him to leave his suitcase and cello. Waiting no longer, he took her to bed.

CHAPTER EIGHT

Claude

What Mariana felt as an absence was, for Claude, a welcome presence. When she led him through the house, he felt that he could *hear* his teacher's voice. In the master bedroom, a pair of suspenders still hung from a hook. Claude smoothed the coverlet lovingly, as if the old man might return for his daily nap. In the dining room, he could almost believe the maestro had just left the table, having eaten the same stew and sipped the wine he and Mariana now shared. The smell of the hallway, the feel of the carpet and wide-plank floors, the texture of the plaster and the wainscoting and curtains—these were things Feldmann had once owned, and now Claude took possession of them too.

The phone rang rarely and no one dropped in. No one knew they were there. Mariana prepared delicious little feasts for two. They drank wine from Alexander's cellar. For lunch, they ate leftovers, on a picnic blanket in the garden, out by the old empty swimming pool. When weather permitted, they napped together in the warm May sun.

Claude, leaving so soon for home, wanted all of her. He wanted her in every room, in every corner of the house. He wanted to absorb everything this week could give him of Mariana and her father, to share and become heir to the legend of this place and its late owner. While he practiced, Mariana sat with him, at his insistence, and critiqued his playing. He wanted every last drop, every last bit of musical insight, channeled from his master through his master's child.

Each afternoon they went for sunlit rambles through the sweet-smelling grounds, resplendent with birds and blossoming lilacs and lilies of the valley. Only when Mariana withdrew each day to a far corner of Swann's Way, out of his hearing, to play the Vuillaume, was he alone. Then he checked his cell phone, taking note of the many calls from his mother and the few from Sophie. He did not return them. He wanted no interruption, no more than what he had here. It would so soon be over.

Toward the end of the week, Mariana received a call, an invitation from Tanglewood to dinner at the Koussevitzky mansion, a "prelude" supper for donors and sponsors to inaugurate the season. They were sorry to invite her so late, they said. They'd only just learned that she was back at Swann's Way. Claude, hearing about the invitation, suggested it could be fun to go to the party together. "When will it be?" he asked.

"The weekend after you leave," Mariana said wistfully. "It's really too bad. I'd so like the Tanglewood brass to meet you."

"But do you think I would be welcome to go with you?"

"Of course. You're Claude Roselle, Feldmann's foremost student."

Was she mocking him?

But Mariana took his hand. "I *do* wish you could come."

This made him think. He really didn't need to be back in Switzerland so soon. After all, he had been practicing here, and her coaching was invaluable. He might perhaps meet the people who could engage him for a concert here in Tanglewood. Claude decided he would postpone his departure. He reserved a new return flight to Lugano to buy himself ten more days at Swann's Way. Somehow he would have to explain this to his mother and to Sophie as well.

"I feel I've gotten a reprieve," Mariana told him. "Ten more days before the noose!" Her joy gave him pleasure. Perhaps, he thought, I share this joy. Am I falling in love?

❧

The Koussevitzky mansion sat on a ridge five miles from Swann's Way. Cars lined the driveway. It was dusk by the time they arrived. Claude held her waist as they looked at the expansive view, the breadth of the Berkshires and sky-piercing silhouettes, around the parapet where they stood.

They were warmly welcomed. No one had seen Mariana in months. She made introductions: "My father's gifted student, Claude Roselle. He's visiting to help me with Alexander's papers and music manuscripts. We have to make some sense of what he left behind. I hope someday you'll hear Claude play."

They had of course heard of him, and several owned his recordings. Two of the guests had even been present at Alice Tully Hall when he performed the Brahms sonatas with William Rossen. Claude was gratified. They not only knew of his New York debut but also had long heard from Feldmann about "his young Swiss disciple." To Claude's surprise—Mariana had not warned him—the gift of the Silver Swan had now been made public. Over and over, they were congratulated—he for his good fortune and she for her generosity. Mariana answered that this choice—hers and her father's—had been the right thing to do. "Alexander had a horror of seeing instruments locked up. Put out to pasture, he called it."

At dinner they sat at a table for eight with officials from the Boston Symphony Orchestra and the music festival. Toasts were proposed to Feldmann's memory. They would miss Alexander, they said. Somewhere up above, someone joked, the maestro was no doubt looking down on them, disdaining their opinions and the wine. This would be the first year in fifty that Feldmann was absent, though, they insisted, not forgotten, never forgotten. They would name a scholarship in his honor, or a cello competition, and try to extract, from this incomparable loss to the world of music, at least a little gain. They expected Mariana to remain in the community, attached to the Music Center. They hoped that Roselle would return. He would be welcome back. Claude felt he had entered the inner sanctum of the world he so wanted to conquer.

Across the table, Mariana was radiant. Claude took pleasure in watching her and listening as she teased and entertained the men on either side. They vied for her attention. She was at home among old friends. A distinguished older man pulled up a chair beside him, and Claude turned. "I hope you will consider playing for us at Tanglewood, M. Roselle."

"It would be my pleasure," Claude answered, "whenever you invite me."

❧

Dinner ended at eleven, and they drove back to Swann's Way. Exuberant, he told Mariana he had been asked if he would be available to perform with the BSO in the summer of 2012. It would be his first appearance at the festival; his manager would fix the date and terms. "It's wonderful, darling," Claude said. "Really, you've done this for me. For so many reasons, I'm in your debt. Now let me do something for you. What will it be?"

Without hesitation, she answered, "Come back to me after your next tour. I'll open Swann's Way for the summer and we can be together." She smiled at him, a very slight smile that seemed to him to bear a hint of a challenge. She dropped her right hand from the wheel to fondle his left. "Perhaps I should think about keeping Swann's Way. For us."

He felt a sudden chill. Leaning back, he stared out into the darkness. Mariana, it seemed, was envisioning a life with him, making plans for a shared future in America, even after he'd been so forthright with her in New York about his intention to remain unattached. He would never live in America. His home was Europe, he belonged in Switzerland. Could he even contemplate a life with Mariana, wherever it might be?

He helped her out of the car and they made their way to the house, hurrying up the front steps. Claude pulled Mariana into the living room and down onto the sofa, where they made love in the dark. After, seized with confusion, he held her while she slept.

❧

When he awoke in the morning, he wondered how and when they'd climbed the stairs. Mariana lay beside him, naked, but he had no memory of leading her, nor of being led, up the long staircase and down the corridor. A thick fog encased the mountains. The air was damp and cool. He slipped out of bed and put on his robe. In the kitchen, he brewed coffee. Then he called his mother to tell her the wonderful news about the BSO.

Francine was pleased. After they'd talked for a minute, she said, "You must come home now, Claude. You've stayed away too long. There are things that must be decided."

"What things?"

"I can't discuss them on the phone. Please, *Liebchen*, come home at once."

"What kind of things?" he asked again.

She was silent. He could picture her—the phone cord wrapped around her wrist, a cup of chamomile tea at her side, the *infusion* she took after lunch—in the chair by the bay window. She would be crocheting, perhaps, or reading the newspaper or polishing her nails.

"I have really enjoyed Swann's Way, Maman. Alexander always spoke of it so glowingly. He was right. It's very special. I'm regaining my energy."

"I've never been there," Francine said dryly. "You must tell me about it."

Claude's last day with Mariana was elegiac. They walked the now familiar trails, practiced their celli in separate rooms, and shared a bottle of Pommard at dinner on the porch. All night they talked and made love, and he consoled her, promising, "We'll see each other soon again."

❧

The next morning they drove to Boston. At Logan, Mariana dropped him off without parking the car. They kissed as the policeman insistently waved her away from the curb, yelling at her to move on. Claude watched with sadness as she pulled away. Then he picked up his cello and suitcase and walked through the automatic doors, on his way home to his work.

CHAPTER NINE

Mariana

Mariana drove back to Stockbridge. She had packed her bags when Claude packed his, planning to return to Swann's Way only to pick up her Vuillaume, collect the papers she had promised Baum, and close up the house. On the radio, she listened to Murray Perahia play Schubert impromptus. She wanted terribly to feel calm. Claude had promised they would meet within six weeks.

Finishing her various tasks at Swann's Way, depleted and lonely, she decided to spend the night at the Red Lion Inn on the main street of Stockbridge. She reserved a single table for dinner at seven. This comforting old place, with its rocking chairs on wraparound porches, its many chimneys and antique charm, had been a favorite of her parents'. They had eaten there often as a family.

At the front desk she checked in and took the ancient birdcage elevator to the second floor. The walls of her room were papered in an early American flower print with red roses on green vines. There were rag rugs and a fireplace with logs laid crosswise in it. The inn had occupied the corner of Main Street for more than two hundred years. Here, she felt safe. She stripped and ran a bath. The tub was deep, if short, with claw feet and old-fashioned faucets. She sank back to soak, stretching her legs over the rolled enamel lip, letting her toes drip water onto the floor. Although the hot scented bath soothed her body, her mind would not quiet. Should she tell Claude about his mother's affair with her father? Why should she be the bearer of this news which, were he to know, would make him so unhappy?

In fact, here was something good that had come out of all the misery. After Pietovsky left, it had seemed unlikely she would allow herself ever again to feel so deeply. And now she was beginning to realize that Claude had awakened her. Her body had come alive: she was falling in love with him.

Her cell phone rang. Shaking soapy water off her fingers, Mariana picked it up from the three-legged stool by the tub.

"Hello, my love."

"*Claude...*"

"My plane has been terribly delayed. I'm still in the club at Logan and I've been thinking of nothing but you. I already miss you. Where are you now?"

"At the Red Lion Inn. In the bathtub." How affectionate he was at this distance.

"Oh, God," he groaned, "and I'm in an airport lounge."

"I decided to stay a night here to savor every moment of our time together."

"And that's what I'll do on the plane..."

"Next time I'll bring you to the inn and introduce you to my father's favorite waiter. He's almost as old as Alexander was, and his hands shake. Don't order soup. The bowl arrives empty by the time he gets it to the table." She stopped. "Oh, Claude, when will I see you again?"

"We won't wait long."

"But when?"

"As soon as my schedule makes it possible, my darling."

After they said goodbye, Mariana stepped out of the tub, dried herself off, and climbed into the canopied bed. The light was fading as she fell asleep.

*

At dinner, Mariana was one of the few guests who chose to eat outside. Seated at a small table in a circle of light, she ordered an old-fashioned and picked up the menu. She drew her shawl around her shoulders. The evening was growing chilly.

One year before Alexander died, they had come here together to eat in the main dining room. Mariana had held her father's elbow and helped him up the porch stairs. Stooped, he used his cane. They made slow progress. It was January, and Main Street sparkled in the snow. Few people had ventured out. In the last years, before Alexander stopped leaving the house, their trips to the Red Lion Inn had been more a ritual observance than a meal. Alexander barely ate. His appetite, he liked to say, for everything but music was just about used up. Still, they ordered drinks and shared an early dinner while the staff fawned over him, pointing to his signed photo in the reception room, saying how well he was looking and inquiring what he was up to these days. He visibly brightened. He listed the names of his students and how far they traveled to sit at his feet. He named the countries they came from, the concerts they were giving, the competitions they won. The waitresses would flatter him: "Still so tall and handsome, Mr. Feldmann. Still so very active." Old narcissist that he was, Alexander reveled in these exchanges.

Mariana could almost feel the energy he absorbed from the attention. For a moment he would cease complaining about the difficulties of old age, the slights to his amour propre, his failing sight.

"You're ninety, Papa," she would say. "Of course your eyes are deteriorating. So are mine, and I'm not yet forty."

"A mere child."

"In your eyes only, and your eyes are, by your own admission, not very good." She clinked his glass with hers. "Your health."

"Oh, Mariana, you have no idea—no idea of what it feels like to be ninety. I'm alone in my generation, my friends are all dead and your dear mother's no longer beside me." He paused for effect. "At least I have my ears."

"Which would be better," she scolded him, "if you wore those damn six-thousand-dollar hearing aids you insisted on buying."

"I can hear music without them. What else do I need to hear?"

"You'd hear what I say to you."

Her father laughed. "Yes. Now there's a good reason to throw them away."

⁂

These insults were lighthearted and loving. This hadn't always been so. He had been hard on her and demanding. At first, he said he wouldn't be her teacher, he was too often away. When he decided no other teacher would suffice, he took over. He couldn't bear it when his criticism of her playing, which he offered profusely, made her cry. It made him furious. Did she not understand the gift that he was offering? Didn't she know a great artist had to be tough? He offered parsimonious praise and was quick to criticize any musical ideas she had that were not his own or that he guessed came from Starker.

With his public, Alexander had great charm and wit. With his students, he offered support, lending his instruments and money, writing recommendations for jobs, preparing them for recitals, and often inviting them to Swann's Way in the summer. But when it came to lessons, he was stern. He had been capable of great cruelty, his temper volcanic. He would say anything that came into his head, however mean. He refused to be challenged or contradicted, demanding respect and obedience. She had frequently overheard him in his studio; he was imperious, harsh and tactless, but always, always right. His students both revered and feared him; they returned again and again, and from great distances, to learn.

But he was not *their* father. The decision to become a first-rank soloist had been made for her, Alexander claimed, because of her great talent, and she had to bear the responsibility for it. "I gave you this talent," he would proclaim. "Don't throw it back in my face!" And once, during a particularly challenging lesson, when she had dared to resist his advice, he had said, "I never wanted you. I didn't want a child. You've been nothing but an albatross—something your mother needed." This had burned into her brain, unforgettable.

Over time, his pronouncements confused her. Alexander would say that women were simply not as musically gifted as men—women were never meant to have important careers in music. They didn't have the creativity or endurance. The life was too hard. They couldn't be happy or fulfilled without a husband and children. "Of course you're a special case," he would conclude. "You're my daughter—a chip off the old block. The two of us are birds of a feather. Cut from the same mold."

In his last years, she read to him when his eyes failed. Little in the realm of literature interested him, but he asked to be read the news and the Arts section of the *New York Times* each day. They would wince over bad reviews of musicians they knew and even those they didn't know, if the review was nasty enough to evoke sympathy.

"Who would do this, Mariana?" Alexander would say irritably. "Who would want to be a musician? You work for years, your entire childhood, you master an instrument and practice every day of your life in order to be told by some moron that you aren't any good, or if you once were, you aren't anymore, or that your interpretation of such and such was shallow, too fast, too slow, off-key. You feel humiliated and furious, but there's nothing you can do. And who, anyway, was the idiot who wrote this review? Someone who used to write for the sports page!" He practically spat with contempt. "Ach, it is a terrible business. You put your head aboveground merely to be shot at."

Mariana sighed. He didn't mean it. He was well aware of the rewards to be reaped from a successful career in music.

"You have to be strong. You have to rise above the petty criticism," he continued accusingly. She rolled her eyes. Although he'd received few bad reviews in his lifetime, he could remember every biting word of each one, verbatim—they continued to rankle, forty or fifty years later. "You were never strong enough, sweetheart. You had no confidence. You should have been more like me. Tough."

"I should have," she agreed.

"I don't know what happened to you," he would say, shaking his head sadly.

⁂

At first bold and confident onstage, Mariana had begun, in her late twenties, to lose her self-assurance. The pleasures of travel diminished. The pressure of performance, the constant stream of strangers who joined her for late suppers after concerts and engaged her in meaningless conversation, the men who tried to seduce her—all this took away from her desire to pursue a large international career, as did her father's ruthless criticism of her concerts he attended, although they were not many. He was occupied with his own schedule and, in addition, refused to attend any concert of hers at a hall where he himself had not been engaged. Mariana faced concerts with increasing dread. After Anton left her, she began to experience paralyzing terror before each performance, a dizzying panic. Black shapes clouded her vision. Her heart hammered in her chest. Nothing helped—not psychotherapy, medication, standing ovations, or spectacular reviews.

In the winter of 2002, Mariana traveled alone to Washington, D.C., to perform the Dvořák concerto with the National Symphony, her first major concert since Pietovsky had gone back to his wife. Although her father had offered her the Swan for the concert, Mariana had chosen to play the Vuillaume. Increasingly superstitious, she followed ever more elaborate rituals, which both reassured her and made her feel as if she were crazy. She packed her gown in the same three dry cleaner bags, tied with velvet ribbon; she placed familiar objects next to the bed in her hotel room; she ate only certain foods at certain times and read the same poems aloud the afternoon before she was to play. She had been prescribed beta-blockers to help her remain calm, but she would not take them, sure they would make her less focused and more forgetful.

In Washington, the morning rehearsal went well. The conductor was sensitive to her playing and complimented her interpretation. The concert hall was empty and the mood relaxed. She had played the Dvořák many times. But as the afternoon passed, she felt she was losing control.

That evening, as she strode onto the stage, cello in hand, wearing a bold red dress, she felt a wave of vertigo. The lights were too bright, the stage tilted. It was terrifying. Confused, she stopped and balanced on her instrument. The orchestra members had turned to watch her entrance and the audience rose to welcome her. Trying to regain her composure, she went directly to her chair without shaking hands with the concertmaster and conductor, a terrible breach of custom. She was breathing hard. The conductor waited till she raised her bow, giving him a signal to begin. Two minutes into the concerto, she lost her way in the music and couldn't find it again. Mariana was drenched in perspiration. The conductor halted the orchestra and looked at her with concern, suggesting they pick up the music at an agreed upon measure. Again, they started and again she lost her place. She couldn't hear the orchestra, so loud was the roaring in her ears. In shame and distress, she rose to leave the stage, but fainted as she passed along the edge of the violin section. Someone caught her cello as she slipped to the floor. The music world was electrified by news of the failed concert. Mariana was rushed to the hospital, where after a thorough exam the doctors could discover no physical problem. They diagnosed an acute panic attack and recommended medication, which Mariana refused.

Alexander was in Europe, to her great relief. She returned to New York and went directly to her parents' apartment, unable to return to her own, alone. She entered quietly, put down her suitcase and cello, and went to her mother's room. Pilar lay in a hospital bed, a pale sun on her thin face, the oxygen tubes affixed. Her afternoon nurse sat quietly in a chair near the bed while Pilar slept, but when Mariana came into the room, she rose to stand by her side.

"Your mother's not doing well, Miss Mariana," she said. "She's more than ever confused and her breathin's bad. I'm glad you came home." Then she left the room.

Mariana pulled up a chair and leaned her head on Pilar's bed. She took her mother's hand in her own and, getting no response, began to sob. "Please listen. Please help me, Mama. I need you." She searched her mother's face and spoke more urgently. "Listen to me. I need help. Mama, I want to die. Papa will be so ashamed of me. I'm so ashamed of myself, I'm such a failure. I've disgraced you both."

Pilar's eyes opened. She stared vacantly at her daughter and patted her hand before once again falling asleep.

⁂

The ancient waiter brought Mariana her old-fashioned, limping across the dining room to where she sat alone. She remembered helping her father to the men's room, that last time they'd come for dinner, and waiting for him outside the door. He had taken a long time and, at last, asked her to come inside. "I've sprung a leak, Mariana," he confessed. "What shall I do? Do my pants look terrible? She made him turn slowly around in the bathroom's bright light and reassured him no one would notice. She saw a small, moist stain on his left thigh.

"It's nothing, really, Papa. No one will see. But perhaps you would feel more confident wearing something like Depends when we go out—for your own sake, so you don't have to worry."

He looked at her, eyes flaming. "Never. Never."

"Say it three more times, and you'll be quoting King Lear." But the reference was lost on him, and he did not laugh.

Back at their table, Alexander took her hand. "You know how much I love you, my dear, and how grateful I am for your help. You are my sweet daughter. Where would I be without you? You've always been the center of my life."

Give him half a martini, she thought, and he became a sentimentalist. But, Mariana told herself, beggars can't be choosers. Just as she had with her mother, she would take what affection was offered and try to believe in it. She raised her glass to him. It was their last dinner at the inn.

❧

Back in Manhattan the week after Claude left, Mariana met with Heinrich Baum. He had left her a message, inviting her to dine at Bella Rosa, a fashionable restaurant on Lexington Avenue. At eight that evening she found him perched on a stool at the bar, sipping a glass of wine. He waved as she entered. She joined him.

"I'm glad to see you. What will you drink?"

She ordered a sidecar. After the silence in Stockbridge, the echoing din of the crowd at the bar assaulted her.

"I'm sorry about the Swan, Mariana. I've just been to an auction where an Amati violin received a record-breaking price. These great instruments become only more valuable."

"Well, let's hope the newer instruments do as well." She handed him the folder of papers listing all the copies of the Swan, and they went over the value and merits of each. After a second drink, Baum put his arm around her and asked — they were, after all, old and intimate friends — if she might like to go to bed with him. It wasn't the first time he'd asked.

"Oh, goodness, Hanns, you're taking advantage of an orphan." Laughing, she pushed him away. "Anyway, it would be like sleeping with an uncle! Interesting but ill-advised."

"Such scruples, Mariana," Baum answered irritably. "You've always seemed to like older men."

"Go to hell, Hanns," she snapped. The maître d' invited them to their table. Mariana, storklike, strode ahead of the instrument dealer. They were shown to a semicircular booth where they sat back on the plush red leather cushions. A waiter asked if they would like another round; she declined. Hanns had something on his mind, she could tell, and she wanted to keep a clear head. "Just water, please."

Baum, recovering his dignity, ordered a bottle of Puligny-Montrachet. At last, having studied the menu, he said, "You know, there were rumors about your father..."

"Yes?"

"About his affairs. Surely you heard them as you grew up. He was very appealing to women, very charismatic. He was known to be a roué. People always talked, but no one could be sure what was true."

"Yes, isn't it curious?" She looked away from him. "People always seem intrigued by the sex lives of artists — the famous ones. I don't know why they find it so fascinating. If my father had had all the affairs people claimed, he would have had no time at all to play the cello. It's idle gossip and it was hurtful to my mother."

"I'm only worried about you. You've lost something that was always intended to be yours, Mariana. How will you provide for yourself?"

"I have his accounts, his assets, and his property in the Berkshires. He didn't leave me poor. I'll be okay. I'll return to teaching." She touched his hand with hers. "Hanns, this really is none of your business. Your job is to sell the copies."

"Fine. But please do tell me when you decide it *is* my business. I'll be waiting." Baum signaled to the waiter. "Would you like to order, my dear?"

⁂

Mariana brought dinner to an end as quickly as she could, claiming exhaustion. She had not slept well since Claude left. He had not called. Walking up Lexington Avenue to shake off the unpleasantness of the evening with Baum, she passed the 92nd Street Y. In the fall before his ninetieth birthday, Feldmann had been honored by friends and musicians at a concert there. Every seat was filled. A film was shown about his life and career—a film in which he failed to mention the existence of Pilar or Mariana. At midnight she and her father rode back to their hotel in a taxi. He had drunk too much champagne. "Sweetheart," he declared, patting her knee, "all my life I've wanted only *one* thing for you."

Mariana held her breath. What had he wanted? Had she succeeded or failed in gratifying his wish?

"I wished for you," he finished, "that before I died you would see me honored the way I was tonight, and you would know how greatly I have been esteemed."

CHAPTER TEN

Claude

Built of glass and steel, Claude's apartment building towered over the stone structures of old Lugano. Claude greeted the concierge as he strode into the lobby. He took the elevator to the twelfth floor, extracted the apartment key from his cello case, and unlocked the door, dropping his bag and raincoat in the foyer. Standing his cello against the Steinway—on which were arrayed stacks of music and one crystal goblet, the dregs of dried red wine in its bowl—he felt glad to be home. He had been away for well over a month.

The room was alight with morning sun, its large plate-glass windows unshaded. Two chairs with music stands stood adjacent to the piano, reminding him that he'd been playing piano trios the day he left for Boston. How much had changed since then.

The flight, once it departed, had been uneventful and he'd slept through much of it, but he felt weary. Francine, as promised, had arranged a car service for him at Malpensa Airport. He wanted to rest and shower before joining his parents for lunch in Montagnola. So many people—Mariana, Sophie, his mother, his father, his manager, his friends, his concert audience—demanded his attention. Claude, burdened by all their expectations, craved time alone.

He drank flat Pellegrino from an open bottle in the refrigerator. On the marble counter by the sink he found a note from Gina, his maid, written in her childish hand: "Sir, I have answered the phone when I was here because it ring so much. I thought it must be you calling me, but it was Miss Sophie. Your father also call to say he cannot meet you for lunch tomorrow when you come back. You must telephone at his studio. Welcome home."

He sighed, exasperated. Francine would be at the house by herself. He'd get the third degree. He dragged his suitcase into his bedroom and spilled its contents out on the floor. The bed had been impeccably made, its duvet smooth as glass. He lay down.

Try as he might to sustain interest in the lives of others when he was not in their presence, Claude was apt to be forgetful. He realized this was a shortcoming, but it was hard to correct. What was in his head when he was on his own was only music, cello technique and the demands of his most immediate travel and performance. With the cello, he lived his fullest life. Perhaps because he'd been an only child, and his parents were not young, it had been his closest companion. He had started young and become so quickly caught up in his music studies, he knew he'd missed some other parts of his youth. For whatever mysterious reasons one young person chooses music and finds a lifelong passion while another begs to be freed from it, Claude's commitment had been clear by the age of five. Throughout his early years, when the rewards were private—untold hours, practicing alone in his room—he never longed to be elsewhere, never looked at the clock except to make sure he'd left enough time for his homework and the dull demands of school.

These were the hours he cherished, and his effort was rewarded by every improvement he heard in his playing. Other boys scored goals, served aces, sped down the Alps on skis, or excelled in class. Claude lived for the cello, his lessons, the chance to play chamber music at the conservatory and sit first stand in the orchestra. He traveled the city of Lugano with the instrument strapped to his back, hearing music in his head, practicing phrases on his leg as he stood on the bus or ferry, train or tram. Because he was handsome and easygoing, he never lacked friends, though he had little time for them unless they were musical as well. Together they would talk shop, listen to recordings, critique performances, and discuss technique the way other boys talked of football matches.

Once he began to perform, the rewards became more tangible: the attention and applause, the money and excitement of travel, the beginnings of a career and his power to move people with his playing. But his interest in people went only so far.

Why had he been relieved to say goodbye to Mariana? It wasn't that he wanted to leave her, he decided, but that he was ready to return to work. He wasn't accustomed to intimacy. As his career enlarged, so too had his expectations of himself and his certainty that he had no room in his life for a partner. He had announced this to Sophie from the start. She had, perhaps, not believed him, waiting patiently for him to change his mind. She had never reproached him, but he'd begun to worry he would hurt her. The possibility of tears, recriminations, explanations quite bored him. When he next saw her, they would have to talk about it. With Mariana, he'd be very careful. Whatever the intensity of his present feelings, he surmised it might be largely about sex.

⁂

The telephone rang. He checked the caller ID on his bedroom phone. It was his father. He would have to answer. Settling back against the pillows, he picked up the receiver. "Papa?"

"Claude. Welcome back."

"It's very good to be home. When did *you* get back to Lugano?"

"Only yesterday. It's always good to be back here."

"I got your message about lunch. I'm sorry you can't join us."

"Yes, I was looking forward to it," said Bernard. "But there's a meeting at the conservatory I'm afraid I can't afford to miss. Dinner, perhaps tomorrow? What's *your* schedule?"

"I was surprised to learn you're here. Maman says you've been busy in Vienna."

"I came to Lugano to celebrate the Silver Swan with you. Isn't it extraordinary?"

Claude stretched. "Totally! I can hardly think of anything else."

"I must say," Bernard continued, "the news came as a surprise to me. Your mother often said Alexander might give you the cello one day—*she* doesn't seem as surprised as I. In any case, it's wonderful news, well worth a trip to celebrate."

"*Grazie.* It was amazing to play the Swan at my New York debut."

I've heard of your great success there. Maman sent me the reviews."

"Yes, the tour went well, though I'm very tired now. Shall we have dinner this evening, Papa?"

"Tomorrow's the day, so I'm told. Maman says you'll be seeing Sophie tonight."

Claude was perplexed. He'd made no date with Sophie. He hadn't even planned to call quite yet. "Tomorrow, then."

"Your mother will arrange everything."

"She always does," Claude said. He was annoyed. Bernard hung up.

Claude showered and shaved. Dressed once more—in clothes from his closet, at last, not his suitcase—he took the elevator to the underground garage. In the dim light, his silver Porsche Targa waited. He coaxed the car into sputtering life, opened the sunroof, and eased it into gear. As the garage door rose, he was momentarily blinded by the noontime sun. He put on his sunglasses, revved the engine, and roared up the steep hills to Montagnola.

⁂

Francine awaited him. As he climbed the stone stairs, she threw open the door. There were flowers in the hall—bright gerberas, his favorite—and the smell of the house was familiar: furniture polish, fresh bread, coffee. Chopin mazurkas played on the old stereo set. The windows had been opened to the summer air. His mother, wearing her striped red-and-white apron, reached up to touch his hair. "You must be tired, *chéri*."

"Yes, I won't stay long today. I need time to sleep."

She drew him into the house. "Really, Claude, your schedule is too busy now. You *must* make time to rest."

He refrained from pointing out that *she* was the one who had made this appointment and kept him from going straight to bed. On the round table in the living room she had arranged a pot of coffee with two china cups and an assortment of pastries: *pain au chocolat*, croissants and jam, slices of cheese. "Since you were in the air all night," said Francine, "I thought you might prefer breakfast to lunch."

"Lovely." He smiled. He was suddenly touched by his mother's thoughtfulness and sank gratefully into a soft chair near the window. Warm sunlight spilled onto his lap. "I've been dreaming of good coffee." She knew the way he liked it—how much sugar, how much milk—and the *pain au chocolat* was warm.

As they ate, she questioned him about his American tour, how he felt about the concerts, the cities he had visited, the people he had met. Her pride in his achievements was so manifest it shamed him to resent her, yet he wished she had a richer life of her own, that her career had flourished, as had his and his father's. They talked about the Silver Swan, her gratitude and his to Feldmann, how soon the restoration work would begin, and when he would return to New York to bring the instrument home.

"And Mariana?" she asked at last.

"She's been very kind to me. Remember, she introduced me to the management at Tanglewood and the BSO."

"Yes, that was another stroke of luck." She poured more coffee. "But as Feldmann's student, you would have come to their attention anyhow."

"Perhaps. But not as quickly." Claude saw little purpose in continuing to talk about Mariana. Something about the woman agitated his mother; that was clear. She set out fruit and nuts. He peeled an apple and offered her a slice.

"Claude, you know I've been waiting to talk to you."

"Yes, I know, but I haven't a clue why. What's worrying you? Ever since you insisted I come home so urgently, I've been nervous. Are you all right? Is Papa?"

He had not in truth been all that concerned but thought it best to say he was. His mother often dramatized things. Now she pressed her fingertips together. "Really, it should be Sophie who tells you the news. I've decided it's not up to me, I must only tell you that you need to go see her immediately."

"Oh, God," he joked, "has she found another boyfriend? Someone who stays in Lugano all the time and attends to her?"

"Don't be silly. I'm not joking."

"Has she taken a job in another country? Perhaps China?" He felt this might be good news.

"Stop, Claude, this is serious. She called me, quite upset, when she hadn't heard from you for more than two weeks. I said you were at Tanglewood arranging future concerts and would be home soon. I didn't tell her you were there with another woman."

"Why?" He sipped his coffee and eyed his mother over the cup's rim. "Mariana's scarcely 'another woman.'"

"I urged her to wait until you came home to have your conversation. I thought that would be better..."

"What conversation?"

"Listen, my darling"—she pursed her lips—"I'm trying to stay out of your personal life, as I always do. This is why I'll let Sophie speak for herself, but you haven't many days by now to be here at home. And you'll have much to think about. You must call her immediately."

When, he wondered, had his mother ever tried to stay out of his personal life? He studied her. In the bright morning light she looked weary, her face lined.

"You'll call?"

He tried once more to challenge her. "Do I really need to call? I understand you've already arranged for us to dine together tonight. Have you also made a reservation?"

"Don't be ridiculous. I simply told your father that he and I won't have dinner with you this evening because you'll be seeing Sophie. I haven't telephoned her. That's for you to do."

Claude shrugged. Rising to leave, he hugged Francine. "Okay, Maman, you win. I'll call her as I'm driving home. I always do just as you say."

She walked him to the door and watched as he loped down the stairs and folded himself into the Porsche. "Thanks for a perfect meal," he called, and waved. Starting up the engine, he drove off.

⁂

Lake Lugano glistened below as he wound down into the city. Ferries and sailboats crossed the water, and the mountains wore a necklace of bright clouds. He turned northeast along the lakefront, heading for the Thyssen-Bornemisa Collection, where Sophie worked. Passing his apartment building, he lamented his lost chance to take a nap.

From the car, he called Sophie's office. Her secretary answered and, after a moment, connected him. He could picture Sophie at her desk in the beautiful old mansion, with its leaded windows giving out over the lake, the art books and catalogs on shelves, the watercolors and oil paintings arranged on the walls. The back of her antique chair, he knew, rose high behind her head.

"Yes, this is Sophie von Auer."

"It's Claude. I've just returned. Do you have any time

now? I heard from my mother that you have something to tell me."

"Welcome home," she said, her voice crisp. "Yes, I thought I might hear from you today. Where are you?"

"I've just arrived in the museum parking lot."

"Oh, Claude." She laughed. "I'll ask Tya about my appointments. I hope I'll be able to meet you."

Ten minutes later, half asleep, he heard her high heels approaching the Porsche. She walked briskly, dressed in a chic gray suit and carrying a briefcase. With her dark blond hair swept up in a chignon, she looked every inch the professional woman. Slipping into the car beside him, she turned his head toward her and kissed him on the lips.

"How much time do we have?" he asked, turning the key.

"I'm finished for the day. Sudden, terrible headache." She smiled.

"Then Gandria, perhaps?"

"Why not? It's a lovely afternoon."

Instantly he regretted having suggested the shoreline village. It was the site of their first tryst two years earlier and would have sentimental connotations for her. On that night, after dinner at the Hotel Moosmann, on the lake's edge, he had suggested they stay the night. Looking up at him over her cup of espresso, Sophie had said, "Yes, why not?" She had impressed him with her frank, direct sexuality, the way she'd taken off her clothes and folded them over the chair by the bed, the way she made no fuss about the details of seduction, the soft intake of breath when she came, and the way, after sex, she rose to brush her teeth. He noticed she had packed a toothbrush in advance.

Now she took a scarf out of her briefcase and tied it tightly around her hair. She put on her sunglasses and fastened her seat belt as well. Claude drove east. The wind and the roar of the engine made it difficult to talk. He wondered again if she had been offered a new job in some other city or country. That would be as good a way as any to bring their affair to a close. Given the unexpected appearance of Mariana in his life, it did feel like the right time.

The road followed the curve of the mountains, emerging from shadow into sun and back again. At Gandria, they parked along the roadside and descended the steep stone stairs through the old village, to the lake.

❧

"I'm glad to see you, Claude. I began to think you weren't going to return." She took a sip of her wine. "How long will you be here?"

They were sitting in the shade of the café's terrace, empty in early afternoon. A rowboat, tied to the iron railing of the terrace, slapped against the wet stone wall beneath. Above them the village clung to the cliff. Claude felt tired, and the wine made him dizzy.

"Not long. I leave on tour next week. First France, then Germany."

"I hear you've been given the great Stradivarius. It's an enormous honor that Alexander Feldmann left his instrument to you. I'm happy for you. When may I see it?"

He brushed away a fly. "I can hardly believe it yet myself. I don't yet have it here with me. The great luthier in Manhattan—Pierre Fernand, the one I mentioned—is doing restoration work on the instrument, work he promised M. Feldmann he'd do. It hasn't been attended to for years and it won't be mine until he's done."

With characteristic directness, she asked, "Was it hard for you with his daughter?"

"What do you mean?"

Sophie broke a breadstick in two and handed him half. "Your mother mentioned that she wasn't happy about the gift."

His mother had broken her promise. "Yes, it was quite difficult. That's why I stayed," Claude lied.

She smiled. Not for the first time he noticed her smile. She had the close-mouthed, tooth-hiding smile that signaled good manners in Europe. In America, by contrast, you could see a person's dentures and cavities and fillings every time someone laughed.

"I don't blame you. It was kind that you stayed on. But it was an unfortunate period for you to be so long away. It complicates things now."

"Ah, yes, your news. My mother said you had news."

A powerboat started its engines at the mooring of the next café. There was a loud thrumming, a backwash, a song on the boat's radio. She waited till the noise subsided.

"I'm almost nine weeks pregnant with our child."

Claude, leaning closer, caught his breath.

"I've known now for a month. I could have told you while you were in America, but it seemed better to wait. You were so focused on your concerts and I didn't want to tell you over the telephone. Anyway, you stopped calling."

He stared at her, speechless. Putting down his wineglass, he drank water. Sophie watched him, her expression neutral.

"Have you told your parents?" he managed.

"Of course not, they'll be appalled. In any case, I thought you should know first."

"Will they be very shocked? Could they possibly think you've never slept with anyone? My God, you're thirty years old."

She smiled. "It isn't that at all. It's that they would hope I'd have more sense than to get pregnant *before* I'm married. That's what will disappoint them. They'll think I've been irresponsible."

Claude looked out over the lake. The houses on the far shore were bathed in afternoon sun. A wave of fatigue swept over him. This was not at all the news he'd expected. "Are you certain that you want this child?"

"*Our* child," she corrected him.

"Our child."

"I'm ready," she said soberly. "Yes, I'm certain that I'll keep it. I am, after all, Catholic."

He was silent again, trying to find something to say. He wanted to say, "How the hell did we two grown-ups let this happen?" Finally he asked what she had told his mother.

"I told her the truth," said Sophie. "When you decided to stay on in America, I asked her how to reach you by phone. She didn't have a phone number, and you weren't answering your cell. I called many times."

The waiter approached. Claude waved him off.

"Your mother could tell I was upset, so she invited me to lunch. I was afraid you'd met someone in America. I know how ridiculous that sounds, but I was in such a state."

He took her hand. "Of course you were." He didn't want to ask about his mother's response. He desperately wished she didn't know.

"I'm aware this isn't a good time." Sophie's voice began to quaver. "A good time to give you my, *our* news. You're going to be leaving soon, you're tired, and you have concerts to prepare. But I haven't really any choice. I'd hoped for more time together." She withdrew her hand from his and regained her composure. "In any case, Claude, I must know if we will get married. If we're going to, I would rather do it soon, obviously."

Feeling trapped, he wanted to flee, to knock over the table and bound up the stairs. At thirty-seven, on the brink of international success, major opportunities and engagements, he did not want to marry or have a child. His feelings for Sophie had not altered or grown since he'd met her. She was a delightful companion, but he had been very clear. Marriage, fatherhood? No, he would be a failure at both. He needed time to carefully phrase his response. As he sat across from Sophie at the small table, he hoped he could conceal his roiling emotions.

Claude took a deep breath. He drank the last of his wine. He knew he had received her news with an absence of joy that must hurt. He spoke softly. "You've had time to think about this, to examine your choices, your conscience, and decide how you feel and what you want to do. I, of course, have not. This comes as a huge surprise to me. I can hardly grasp it. I have no time to grasp it. You've chosen your path, in any case. But I have to prepare for my next concerts. I have to keep my focus—just for a few more weeks."

"And then?" she asked, her eyes welling up.

"I'll finish my tour and we'll figure everything out."

"I understand it is my choice to have this child, Claude, and I don't *expect* anything of you. I only hope we will marry, for the sake of the child and because I love you."

She had never said this before. Devastated, he watched her take a sip of her wine. "For now, Sophie," he said, attempting to smile, "I have nothing more to say." He reached across the table and took her glass. With one swallow, he emptied it. Then he summoned the waiter and paid.

CHAPTER ELEVEN

Mariana

The first days of summer were hot. Claude had been gone for more than two weeks, and Mariana was restless, at loose ends. She thought constantly about him and wondered why he hadn't called, obsessively checking her messages. Sometimes she felt she could hardly breathe, other times she collapsed in tears. Hoping to meet Claude in Europe after he finished his tour, she had checked airfares to Switzerland daily on her computer. Since he had called to report his safe arrival in Milan, he had not called again. She knew he was traveling in France, Germany, and the Netherlands, and tried to remember his schedule. But his silence tortured her. He did not respond to her messages. It was as though he'd dropped off the planet.

Mariana tried to convince herself that his silence meant no more than her father had claimed his silence had meant when he himself went on tour. But then she thought about what Feldmann's silence had in fact disguised, and her anxieties redoubled. Why would he not answer?

Finally, cursing herself for giving in, she went through Alexander's old phone book and found Francine Roselle's number in Montagnola. She placed a call. While the phone was ringing she realized she needed an excuse for calling. Francine answered—"*Allo, Allo?*"—and Mariana, brisk and professional, said, "Hello Mme Roselle, it's Mariana Feldmann. I'm calling from New York. I've got something to discuss with Claude concerning the Tanglewood concert. Can you tell me where to reach him?"

She realized she had made no small talk. She could scarcely bear to speak to the woman. Francine, however, was friendly. "How have you *been*, my dear?"

Mariana forced herself to sound cordial. After they exchanged pleasantries, she inquired again about Claude. Did his mother know his whereabouts?

"I'm not exactly sure where he is today, but you can always reach him on his cell phone. I spoke with him this morning. He was at the airport in Berlin."

She felt a flash of anger. So Claude *was* answering his phone. "We haven't been in touch since he left America. Two weeks ago—nearly three. Is the tour proceeding well?"

"Ah, then, you haven't heard his news," Francine said cheerily. "He would of course want you to know that he and Sophie, his girlfriend, have decided to marry. We are all here very excited. She is a lovely young woman."

"I'm sorry, who?"

"Sophie von Auer. They have been together quite a long time. When he returned from America, they became engaged."

The knife, already lodged in her chest, twisted deeper. Mariana closed her eyes. After a moment she was able to say, "What good news, Mme Roselle. I'm happy for them. When will the wedding take place?"

"Quite soon," she answered. "As soon as he has time. Sophie, of course, must do all the planning, due to Claude's impossible schedule. I'm sure you'll hear from him, but I'll give him the message you called. As you can imagine, he's been tremendously busy!"

Mariana made an effort to sound warm. "Yes, I can well imagine. Thank you and congratulations to your husband as well." They said goodbye and hung up.

⁂

Pilar had called it "playing with fire." That had been her mother's phrase for every level of danger, from climbing on the jungle gym to testing her father's volatile temper to, later on, falling in love. The first time Mariana heard the phrase, it made perfect sense: she was trying to light matches with another four-year-old and, having succeeded, dropped the flaming match on her knee. She had been burned and then punished. That had been playing with fire—the real thing. Later, it was metaphor, and always used to express Pilar's deep distrust of men.

Mariana tried not to lie to herself. The danger of an affair with Claude had been obvious from the beginning. The magnitude of her desire alone had been fair warning that something volcanic had been ignited in her. She had only her reckless behavior to blame. She had had full knowledge, from reading Alexander's letter, of the complications involved: his mother's long love affair with her father, the gift of the Stradivarius, and the simple fact that Claude lived in Switzerland. Small craft warnings had been flying, yet she'd headed out into turbulent water, breathless and compelled.

It wasn't the first time. The object of her very first crush, a swaggering Latvian cellist of twenty-three who studied with

Alexander, had taken her back to his apartment after one weekly lesson to pry her loose from her virginity. She had just turned fifteen. Though determined, he was unsuccessful, and once it was clear that she was too young and frightened, he dropped her, adding insult to injury by patting her on the head and calling her "kid" when he came for lessons. She waited to see him enter the foyer, then wept in her room and plugged her ears to his playing, though she could still hear Alexander shouting, "Ivan, this phrasing is vulgar. Can you be more sensitive? You sound like a gypsy."

Alexander fanned the flames of the distrust engendered by Pilar. He lectured Mariana on the inevitable treachery of men. Men were rash and shallow. They wanted only one thing, and after you gave them what they wanted, they left. If you didn't give them what they wanted, they would leave anyway. Men, he said, were incapable of fidelity. It wasn't in their nature. They cared only about good sex and successful careers. Alexander's message should have alerted her to his own behavior. But what she now understood to have been self-description had seemed, at the time, merely wise and protective and meant to warn her. Only later, when people assumed Mariana was old enough to hear and shed light on the rumors about her father, did she come to realize that he was one of those bastards he had warned her against. He knew the type.

❧

In the moments following her conversation with Francine, Mariana seethed. Her cheeks flushed. She felt dizzy. Claude had been callous, cowardly, and deceitful. Why had he so brazenly lied to her? Her fury quickly turned to anguish.

How could she have so completely misjudged him? Would he marry this Sophie von Auer? Had he not cared for her at all? Could she let him get away with it? Could she allow him to steal her heart *and* her Stradivarius so easily, so carelessly?

The next morning, she telephoned Baum & Fernand. When the receptionist put her through, she said, "Hanns, it's Mariana. Remember the offer you made at Bella Rosa?"

"Which one? I believe I made several."

"The offer to help me."

"I do."

"I'm calling to tell you that the Silver Swan has just become *your* business again. I want it back. You have it."

⁂

They met the next afternoon. Mariana stalked into Baum's office. He did not ask her why she'd changed her mind. She was cold and formal and furious.

"I don't want Roselle to get the Swan," she announced.

"I'm not shocked to hear this." He played with a pen on his desk.

"My father lied to me. He *promised* me the Swan."

Baum was thoughtful. "And what exactly do you have in mind?"

"I want you to sell the cello. Get it out of the country. Sell it to anyone who's willing to keep the cello out of sight for a few years. You can say it has been stolen."

"Claude Roselle *does* own the instrument, my dear."

"Possession's nine-tenths of the law and the cello's right here in your shop."

Baum studied her. "It's highly risky. What you're asking is, of course, nothing short of criminal."

Mariana knew he might well have thought of this idea himself. She had paid attention to talk in the shop when she visited with her father. Baum had made neither his money nor his reputation through simple honesty. She had heard him speak of tax evasion, illegal transactions, and fraud—always about other dealers, of course—of overvaluation, faked pedigrees, and misidentified instruments, but never outright theft.

"Are you interested, Hanns?"

He leaned back in his chair, pressing his fingertips together. "As you can imagine, Mariana, many collectors and cellists—professional and amateur alike—would love to own this cello. It's a rare masterpiece. There are very few comparables. Its value's all the greater because Alexander Feldmann owned and played it. Your father instructed me to find the highest price. He believed there would be a foundation or a private collector in Asia or Kazakhstan or some such place."

"And did you?"

"Yes, I found such a client. This man had planned for several years to buy the Swan and all the copies—excepting the Vuillaume, perhaps—upon your father's death. It was a deal, a fait accompli, we thought, because Alexander led us to believe so."

"Hanns, did you take money from this man in advance?"

"Regrettably, I did. I had formed an understanding with your father when I first lent him money to buy the Swan, years before your birth. We agreed I would receive further money, either from the sale of the Swan or from his estate when he died. Unfortunately for me, we put nothing on paper. I assumed he would honor our agreement since I had made it possible for him to buy the cello at a time when he had no credit."

"So he betrayed you also..."

Baum made no response. She pressed him, "What if he had left it to me and I'd decided to keep the Swan, not to sell?"

"He had assured me in that event, I would be fairly paid by his estate. But when you gave up your solo career, in 2002, your father came to see me. He said he'd changed his will. He would leave the cello to you on the condition that I sell it for you and guarantee your financial security. Since you no longer concertized, he saw no need for you to keep the Swan. He believed it should be heard."

"And what were the terms he offered you?" she asked, her fury rising.

"Thirty percent."

She was certain he was lying. "Did you see the will?"

"No, of course I didn't ask to. I believed we had a gentleman's agreement. We were old friends. And that's when I borrowed a great deal of money, against that future promise, to enlarge my shop and business."

"And now you're angry?"

"I cannot repay my debt."

She crossed her legs. She wondered, briefly, if she could persuade him to join in her vendetta, and what Baum in turn would demand. "And your client? Does he still want the cello?"

"He knows it is not mine to sell, Mariana. And he's not interested in theft. It is too late, we agreed last week when he finally learned that Roselle had been left the Swan."

"What will you do?" she asked.

"I've no idea."

"My father was not a gentleman of his word," Mariana said, rising to leave.

Baum replied bitterly, "I'm afraid that's true."

CHAPTER TWELVE

Claude

Sixteen days later, in Amsterdam, Claude played his final concert of the tour. Once on his way, he had found it easy to block everything from his mind. He concentrated on the repertoire he had to play, the planes he had to catch, the conductors he had to please, and the laundry he washed each night in his hotel room's sink.

Lying in bed in the Sofitel Grand, he ate breakfast and tried to make sense of his reviews in the Dutch morning paper, delivered on his breakfast tray. He looked at the clock; it was six. He wanted—suddenly and urgently—to hear Mariana's voice. It would be midnight or one o'clock in New York. He could never remember time differences. He turned on his phone, found her number, and dialed. After four rings he got her answering machine. Perhaps she was asleep or possibly still at a postconcert party or, a disturbing thought, out with someone else.

"Mariana," he told the machine, "it's Claude. I've just finished my tour. I'm calling from Amsterdam. Where are you and how can I reach you?" After a pause, he heard her pick up the telephone.

"I've missed you terribly," he said into the silence. "I'm sorry I haven't called."

"Claude, oh Claude, at last," she whispered. "I've been frantic. Why haven't you been in touch?"

"I'm sorry. I'd hoped you wouldn't worry. You know touring—the way one loses track of days, weeks. The way one can think of nothing but the next flight, the next concert." He paused, realizing he would have to say more to overcome his inattention. "I thought about you so often, my darling, much to the detriment of my playing, I'm afraid."

"Did you get my messages?"

"Only today," he lied. "When I checked my mobile."

She was silent for a long moment. "I did worry. Of course I worried. I was very sad not to hear your voice." She paused again. "Also, I needed to speak with you about the Tanglewood date. When you didn't answer my calls, I thought perhaps I could contact you through your mother. I telephoned her."

Claude froze. "Ah, did you reach her?"

"Yes. We had a lovely chat, very warm and friendly. But I decided not to leave a message for you. I made the Tanglewood decisions myself."

He stared out the window at the canals of the city, feeling anxious.

"And what were those decisions?"

She ignored his question. "Tell me when I'll see you, Claude."

He tried to think clearly, quickly, sensing something distrustful in her tone. "I've been thinking. If Baum & Fernand will allow me to, I'll come to collect the cello. I've decided I'd like to play the Swan just as it is for a year and then bring it back for restoration. I really want to know the cello as Alexander knew it, to play the instrument he played, before Fernand takes it apart. And if Fernand will agree," he paused, "I'll see you very soon. I'm not sure how much longer I can wait to get my hands on you again."

"I spoke with Baum yesterday. Pierre hasn't been feeling well. I don't think he's started work on the cello yet."

"I'm so sorry to hear about Pierre. I hope he won't refuse me."

"How can he, Claude? You *are* the owner."

"I'll call today."

Outside, the fog was lifting. He had an early flight scheduled out of Schiphol. He hoped planes would be flying by the time he reached the airport.

"Darling," she said into the silence, "I have a wonderful idea. I've wanted for the longest time to return to the Pyrenees, to Prades. Alexander had such fond memories of his years there with Casals, and I haven't been there since I was young. Wouldn't it be marvelous to make a pilgrimage there together?"

Thinking of Sophie and his promise to come home, he answered hesitantly, "I think I could arrange that, for a few days at least. But first I have to return to Lugano and attend to some business there." He paused. "If we meet in Europe, how will I retrieve the Swan, assuming that Pierre agrees to let me have it?"

Mariana laughed. "I've thought of everything. I could bring it to you. I'll fly to Barcelona with the cello. If you meet me at the airport there, we can rent a car and drive together to Prades. It would be a heavenly week."

"I won't have a whole week, Mariana, but even a few days would be special." He lay back on the pillows. "My God, I've longed for you."

She whispered, "Tell me how much. Tell me how you want me. Tell me what you'll do to me on our first night together…and what you want me to do to you."

"Are we having phone sex?" he asked.

"Come on, Claude," she commanded, "don't be such a proper Swiss. Tell me."

⁂

From his apartment, Claude called the offices of Baum & Fernand. Twenty minutes later, Baum returned his call. The dealer was cordial and willing, in Fernand's absence, to agree to Claude's request.

"There's no problem," he declared. "Especially because Fernand himself is not well enough to begin work. His projects are delayed. We will prepare the Swan for you in a new traveling case. Of course when it leaves the shop, you must cover the insurance. Play it for a while, but then, when Fernand is ready, you must bring it back for restoration—it was Maestro Feldmann's wish. When will you come to take it?"

"I believe Mariana Feldmann is planning a trip to Europe," Claude answered. "I thought she might bring it to me. We've discussed this, she and I."

Baum was slow to answer. "Are you sure you wouldn't rather come yourself?"

"I can't see why I should, when she has offered to meet me and deliver the Swan."

"Very well, if you're certain. But there will be papers to sign, M. Roselle, that absolve us of responsibility until you return it to us, and added insurance expenses."

"Of course," Claude answered. "Just fax them to me."

Claude gave Baum his address, his telephone and fax

numbers and, finally, the name of his bank, Union des Banques Suisses.

"Where will you meet Ms. Feldmann?" Baum asked.

"In Barcelona, in ten days."

"Enjoy the cello," said Baum, "and enjoy your visit with the maestro's daughter."

⁂

Before he left for Barcelona, he would have to talk with Sophie, difficult as this encounter would be. Sophie planned to keep the child. He thought it might, in any case, be too late for her to change her mind. She actually *wanted* his child. This made him feel even worse.

He called Sophie's office. "Oh, M. Roselle," her secretary answered, "Ms. Von Auer is not yet back. She was delayed in Vienna at a conference. She won't be back for a week more. She asked me to tell you how to reach her."

Claude said it wouldn't be necessary. He would speak with her in person when she returned. Then he called Mariana and said, "Come right now, Mariana. I have some unexpected free time. Meet me in Barcelona as soon as you can get a flight. Bring the Swan. I've arranged everything with Baum. I have five days."

"I'll use Expedia or one of those other sites, but Claude, the tickets will be ridiculously expensive, if I can even get them. First class, last minute."

"I don't care. I'll pay anything they ask."

⁂

When he met Mariana at the Barcelona airport, she was empty-handed. Hurrying toward him, her hair a tumble of long dark curls, a green leather bag slung on her shoulder, she carried no cello case. As they kissed, he could scarcely contain his anxiety. Where was the Swan and why was it not with her?

Mariana was freshly groomed and radiant. They embraced and he smelled her familiar lilac scent. People moved past them, dragging suitcases, pushing infants in strollers, parting in streams around them. "Have you *just* gotten off the plane?" he asked. "You look as if you've spent the morning at a spa."

She smiled at him. "I'm so glad you noticed the effort I've made. I landed late last night and went to the Ritz."

His anxiety increased. Had she left the cello in her hotel room? "Well, you certainly look irresistible."

They kissed again. "You're not *supposed* to resist me."

Pulling his leather roller behind him, he drew her toward the exit. "I assume you've left the Swan at your hotel. Shall I get us a taxi?"

"No need, I've rented a car—a sweet little convertible. It's in the parking garage." Now *she* led *him* by the hand as they moved into the warm August sun.

"How on earth will we get the Swan and all our bags into a small convertible?"

"We won't, Claude. I've stowed the cello safely at a branch of your UBS bank here in the city. This was Baum's suggestion—we're not staying in very secure hotels and we don't want to carry it everywhere we go. Besides, if I've only a few days with you, I don't want any competition from a cello. I want your undivided attention—all of it, every last caress. You'll play the Swan for the rest of your life—for the moment, you're all mine."

Hoping to hide his disappointment, Claude squeezed her hand. "And you're absolutely sure it's safe?"

"Of course," she answered, with a suggestion of edge in her voice. "But feel free to call the bank if you're worried. You can call to check on your lovely Swan every hour, if you'd like." She handed him a business card from his bank's Barcelona branch, with the name of the branch vice president and a telephone number. "Go ahead."

"That won't be necessary," he answered, trying to be playful. "*You're* a lovely enough swan for me. Let's go quickly. I feel the need to groom your feathers. Are we going to the Ritz?"

"No, I've checked out."

They entered the garage and climbed a dank flight of stairs. She led him to the car, a black Fiat 500c, low to the ground. Planes roared overhead. They could no longer hear each other, and they ceased talking. Putting his bag into the trunk with hers, he climbed into the driver's seat beside her. She looked at him so seductively he wished they were indeed going back to the Ritz, not starting the drive to Prades. On the highway, he asked, "Was it a nuisance—bringing the cello with you?" He couldn't keep himself from returning to the subject.

"Not at all. You forget, I'm quite used to carrying a cello. Actually, I was afraid to bring the Swan to my apartment for even one night. There've been robberies from time to time in my building. Instead, I took a taxi to Baum & Fernand on my way to the airport, and Hanns brought the Strad down to the cab. It's in a beautiful new case, safely locked. I have the key. I'll give it to you after our first night together—if you don't disappoint me."

❦

Vendrell, a village of whitewashed houses and shuttered shops an hour south of Barcelona on the sea, was dusty in the summer heat, even its olive trees drab. Women clothed in black moved slowly through the narrow streets, carrying their baskets. What music they heard blared from boom boxes. Pablo Casals, Feldmann's great mentor, had been born here, but there was little to commemorate him. Two miles farther, however, in the village of Sant Salvador, they visited a museum devoted to Casals.

Here they lingered longer. There was a salon with a bust of the cellist, a cello on a makeshift stage, and rows of crimson chairs. One room held a stone death mask of Beethoven, a few framed measures composed by Brahms, and a lock of Mendelssohn's hair. Mariana was talkative. She seemed nervous and strangely disconnected, he thought, unable to meet his eyes. They ate lunch and drove north through the mountains to Prades.

Casals had lived in exile here when he fled from Franco. Street signs were in Catalan as well as Spanish and French. Their hotel, a small one on the central square, was called the Alchimie. The narrow main street—Avenue Charles de Gaulle—would not have had that name, Claude knew, when Casals and Feldmann walked its length, as he now did with Mariana. At the outskirts of the village, they reached the virtuoso's home, the Villa Colette. Its entrance, disappointingly, was locked. They peered through the gate and then walked back toward the hotel.

At the bar where they stopped for a drink, all the old men claimed to remember Casals, to have known him personally. Some claimed to remember Feldmann as well. They told

Mariana about her father, "Alejandro," who would practice late at night and disturb the other guests. The *patrón* of the bar announced that he himself was seventy-eight and the son of the previous owner. He recounted stories of his father's arguments with Casals's students, some of whom, like Alexander, had lived above this very bar and played too late and too loud. "Alejandro," he winked at Mariana, "was quite a man with the ladies."

❧

Upstairs at the Alchimie, he and Mariana made love. That first night she was passionate. But at breakfast the next morning she seemed withdrawn and disconsolate. He had no idea why.

"Is something wrong? You don't seem happy."

"Do you have something to tell me?" she asked, looking at him searchingly.

"Yes, my sweet, I do. I am very happy to be here with you. I'm glad you proposed this trip."

"Even without the Swan? With no way to practice?"

He felt she was testing him. "Even without it," he lied. "It's *you* I want to be with."

"And no one else?"

What an odd question, he thought, as he poured more coffee.

❧

On their third and final day in Prades, they walked a winding road up Mont Canigou. The homes gave way to olive groves in the commune of Codalet, and then to stone escarpments, until in the distance, finally they could see the tower of the ancient monastery, Saint-Michel de Cuxa. Silent except for the wind and bird cries and, somewhere, the tinkling of belled sheep, the monastery loomed large as they drew near. Even in the August heat, the buildings retained a chill calm. The saint who hallowed Cuxa by sleeping outside on the flat stony ground had had his outline incised in the rock. Built in the ninth century, and rebuilt centuries later, after the leveling rage of anticlerical soldiers, the chapel was a place Casals had often played—a Benedictine retreat made holy for Claude by the thought of his teacher, and his teacher's teacher.

Mariana reminded Claude that she had actually met Casals long ago at the Marlboro Festival in Vermont, when she was a small child. She spoke of her father's deference to his old master, whose hand he kissed repeatedly, deference she had never seen before and never saw again. This legendary artist was part of her family's history. She'd grown up in her father's sophisticated circle, meeting the great artists of the era. Claude was envious. Though it would now be said that he was Alexander's "musical heir," Mariana owned the legacy. He'd received his portion—the Swan—only because she'd stepped aside.

His mind had wandered. Mariana was talking. She told him that a portion of the monastery had been purchased by the American millionaire John D. Rockefeller and transported to America in ships. There he'd rebuilt it at as a museum called the Cloisters at the northern tip of Manhattan. "Can you imagine that?" she was asking. "Moving all these stones across the ocean?"

"Did your parents take you there?"

"To the Cloisters? Never. I went on my own. My father hated museums; they made him feel stupid and they bored him. He knew nothing of art or literature. He cared only about music. Everything else was of no importance. I think in all the years he traveled to Europe to play, he never once walked into a museum." She sounded harsh and contemptuous.

Claude took a stroll alone around the monastery while Mariana sat in a pew in the ancient church. He returned to find her in tears, and he was touched, certain she wept for the memory of her father who had so often played here. He put his arm around her waist. "Let's go back to the hotel. We haven't much time left."

Mariana leaned against him. She asked again, "Do you have anything to tell me?"

"Yes," he repeated. "I have loved these days together—being with you again."

They walked back down the winding road to Prades, arriving in the village just as the church bells began their plangent evening song.

❧

In the Fiat, early the next morning, they sped down the mountain to Perpignan and then south to Barcelona. Both were weary and preoccupied. Claude was returning home to face Sophie and his mother. On the drive he was too tired to talk about the future—when and where they'd meet again. Somewhat to his surprise, Mariana avoided the subject as well. He tried to make her laugh about the endless series of roundabouts—*ronds-points*—the French had created to control traffic. One could barely go five hundred yards without going in a circle. But a curtain had descended. As they crossed the border into Spain, Mariana was silent and pensive. Because her flight to New York left first, at two p.m., she had to be at the airport by noon. Claude, eager to collect the Swan, had urged her to accompany him to the bank—but she did not want to go into the city. She said she feared she'd miss her flight and insisted he drop her off first.

They turned off the highway at a rest stop to have coffee. When he tried to kiss her, she turned her face away. He stroked her hair instead. "What was the Tanglewood matter you called me about?"

"It was nothing, a pretext. I wanted to find you and you weren't answering my calls."

"I wasn't answering *any* of my calls."

"I think there's something you haven't told me." She put her hand on his.

He was again puzzled. "How much I'll miss you?"

She searched his face. "I love you, Claude."

Perhaps that's what troubled her. He hadn't told her he loved her. Suddenly, he wanted to tell her he loved her too, that he too was sad to say goodbye. But would he feel this way next week, next month, next year? Instead he said, "I know. I know you do, darling."

The moment passed. She reached into the green bag at her feet. "The papers for the rental car are in the glove compartment. Here's the key to the new cello case. You'll need it." He took it from her and slipped it into his shirt pocket. They drove on in silence.

⁂

Claude dropped Mariana at the airport, returned the rental car, and went straight to the bank branch office, a gloomy building on the Plaça de Catalunya. He presented himself to the manager, who shook his hand briskly and said it would take a moment to make sure his identity papers were in order before he removed the cello from the vault. He hurried off. Claude paced the tiled floor, trembling with impatience; here at last, alone in Barcelona, he would claim the Silver Swan. The instrument would be his life's companion, his to cherish and protect. Claude felt a surge of joy and gratitude.

The bank manager returned and escorted him to a small private room, with a table and two chairs; there, the instrument case was brought to him. As he undid the locks, excitement made him clumsy. He fumbled with the stiff clasps. The bright blue color of the fiberglass case was too garish for his taste. He would exchange it for something much more dignified—in keeping with the Swan. The case squeaked as he opened it. Tenderly, he removed the soft protective cloth around the instrument as if raising a bride's veil. Then, holding his breath, he unfastened the ribbons that bound her and lifted the instrument out into the light.

Something was not right. He stared. It took several moments before he understood he did not hold the treasured Swan. He could hardly breathe. Laying the cello on the mahogany tabletop, he peered at the label through the f-hole. To his surprise and horror, Mariana had brought him the J.-B. Vuillaume.

Hoping to reach her before her flight took off, he stepped into the hallway and tried to call, but her phone was shut off. There was a knock on the door. The vice president of the UBS office, an elderly Catalan in a black suit with black pomaded hair, introduced himself and asked if everything were satisfactory. Claude, ashen, struggled to answer. "No."

"No?"

"This is not the instrument I expected to receive."

The bank officer stiffened visibly. Rubbing his hands together, he said, "I assure you, sir, this case has not been touched since the señora has delivered to us. We placed it immediately into the vault. Whatever you have found inside is what she has put there for you."

"Perhaps, but I don't understand what happened. I'm not accusing you of anything..."

"I must repeat. Whatever may have happened, Señor Roselle, it does not happen in our bank. Is there anything we can do? Would you like to make a telephone call or contact perhaps the police?"

"No, no," said Claude. "This is not a matter for the *guardia civil*. I'll return to Switzerland and solve the problem there." He replaced the cello in its case and redid the clasps. "I'm sure there's a good reason, and Miss Feldmann will explain it to me when I get back to Lugano."

"You must sign these papers," the man said, "to take it away."

Claude looked at the papers, which simply said "violoncello." Stunned, he signed and left the bank, carrying the bright blue case.

CHAPTER THIRTEEN

Mariana

After Claude deposited her at the Barcelona Airport, Mariana walked straight to the first shop that sold tobacco. She bought a pack of Dunhills, pulled off the cellophane wrapping, and stepped outside to light up. She had stopped smoking more than a decade ago, and she'd made Alexander quit as well. But now she badly wanted a cigarette and felt she deserved it. The first puffs made her so dizzy she had to find a bench to sit on. She smoked two cigarettes. The traffic was constant and loud, the fumes dense. People hurried past.

Claude had been a contemptible coward. He hadn't said one word. She had waited three and a half days—eighty-four hours—for him to work up the courage to confess that he was going to get married. She had even asked, point-blank, if he had anything to tell her. And he said nothing at all. Of course it would have hurt her; he'd had reason to be reluctant. But he owed it to her. His silence was dishonorable, *despicable*, she told herself. What was he planning to do? Send her a wedding announcement? Did he feel nothing for her? She knew she could not have asked him directly without breaking down, losing her dignity and composure. And what if he had lied?

As she approached security, her cell phone rang. It would be Claude, no doubt, calling en route to the bank. She turned off her phone. Let him register *her* silence, as during the weeks of his long tour she had been forced to endure his. She too could play a waiting game. She too could not be reached.

On the plane, Mariana sank into her seat and shifted toward the window, turning her back to the man beside her as if *he* had given her cause for offense. Once she recovered from her affair with Claude, once she had evened the score, she'd be done forever with men. Perhaps there were other kinds of men, but those she knew were contemptible — their ambition, their egotism, their self-love and, above all, their ability to live with lies. Only Anton had been straightforward and honest with her, but he too had cheated on his wife.

Mariana thought, with regret, of her mother's unhappy life. At last, the drone of the plane, now airborne, put her to sleep.

❧

More content in Stockbridge than New York, Mariana's mother had tended her flower garden in her sun hat and shorts. She practiced yoga early every morning and read for hours at a time on the kitchen porch. Zeiss binoculars in hand, she would feed and watch the birds. She could name them all. The phone rarely rang for her; she had few friends and hardly ever went anywhere with her husband. Alexander had built a large addition to Swann's Way, a kitchen wing, full of light, which thrust out fifty feet into the gardens behind the original house, with a porch that ran the length of it. The porch, like those of the old houses in town, had rocking chairs and Pilar's collection of pinecones, gourds, and fronds in large baskets. Over the years, her mother went less and less frequently to Tanglewood, and Alexander hired help for the house so they could entertain. Pilar no longer cooked and refused to give the hired maid and cook any instructions. This was Alexander's job.

Mariana would hear him in the mornings giving orders for dinner, listing what needed to be bought, what sheets would have to be changed, what guests were arriving or departing. As her mother grew more reclusive, Mariana eagerly took up the role of her father's companion during the hectic summer social life of the Berkshires. She attended concerts and parties with Alexander at which he introduced her, without irony, as "the next great Feldmann."

One night, Alexander and Mariana returned from a performance at Ozawa Hall and a postconcert party. It was well past midnight. They came through the door arm in arm, tipsy and giggling like children, to find her mother standing spectral, at the top of the stairs, her face dark and fierce. When they looked up, she turned away, walked down the hall, and slammed her bedroom door.

Alexander, chastened, said, "It's late," and hurried up the stairs. Mariana went to her own room and got ready for bed. Ten minutes later, her mother, wearing a white cotton nightgown, wrenched open her bedroom door and stalked in. Her low voice rasped and her hands shook with rage.

"Listen to me, young lady," Pilar hissed, "I know what you're up to." She pounded her fist on Mariana's bureau. "You'd better stop right now."

"What do you mean, Mama? And why are you so angry? I don't know what you mean."

"Oh, you know all right. You're flirting with your father. You've been doing it for years. You're seductive with him, and he encourages you. It's disgusting—the two of you carrying on, going out together. You're competing with me, your own mother."

Mariana stared at her. "You believe that?"

"Just because you went to college and you play the cello, you think you're better than me. Because you travel around, giving concerts, speaking French, having everyone tell you how talented you are. You think you're so damn beautiful every man is after you. You're young, but you'll get old. It's only a matter of time."

Mariana was horrified. She could think of nothing to say and wouldn't let herself cry. Her mother looked deranged, her hair tangled, dripping gray coils down her back. "That's a terrible thing to say. You're scaring me. Have you been drinking?"

Pilar wasn't finished. "You think just because you play the cello and he puffs you up and tells you how great you are, you think you're really something. You only play to get his attention. Do you think I don't know? I won't have it, young lady!"

"Why do you want to hurt me, Mama? You're hurting me."

Her mother approached, looking straight into Mariana's eyes. "Because you're coming between me and your father. You want me out." Pilar stamped her foot. "But I'm not going. You can't push me out."

"I'm going to get Papa." Bursting into tears, Mariana tried to reach her bedroom door. "*He'll* tell you it isn't true."

"Don't you dare. Don't you dare even talk to him, you troublemaker." Pilar pushed Mariana back against the bed.

"Go to sleep. And mind your own business from now on. Just take care you behave yourself..."

Regally, Pilar stepped through the doorway and walked down the hall to her own bedroom, like a queen approaching her throne. Her nightgown was transparent, and Mariana clearly saw how bone-thin her mother had grown. She closed the door and cried all night, both repelled and appalled by her mother's attack. But in the morning neither mentioned it, and the episode was buried.

⁂

Mariana returned from Barcelona in the middle of the night, hauling her bag up the dark, narrow stairwell, trying not to awaken her neighbors. The air felt hot and stale. She had closed the shades before she left, and now it felt as if she were entering a cave or crypt. Raising the blinds, she switched on the window air conditioners. The light on her answering machine blinked, as she had known it would. Her cell phone, too, registered calls from Claude. She'd let him wait. A bottle of Rémy Martin stood on the table beside the bay window. Next to it stood the Vuillaume's empty case. She poured an inch of brandy into a snifter and took it into her bedroom. Soon, in all her clothes, she fell asleep.

By morning, the apartment had cooled down. Mariana made coffee and listened to her messages, pressing Erase and Skip. The last three were from Claude. She could sense his attempt to control his voice, to be civil and calm—yet he sounded almost hysterical. In the first message he told her that she'd brought him the Vuillaume, not the Stradivarius. Perhaps, in her excitement, she had made a mistake, he suggested. But hadn't Baum himself delivered the Swan to her taxi as she left for the airport? Could she call him, please, the minute she arrived?

In his second message he told her he was leaving for Lugano, carrying the Vuillaume with him, of course. He knew she might not yet be home but hoped she'd call just as soon as she could. By the third message, several hours later, he was desperate. He wondered where she was and why she wasn't answering. He had checked and found out her plane had landed. The shoe was now—Mariana looked at her toes—on the other foot. She erased Claude's messages, showered, dressed, and went out to have breakfast at the diner on the corner. Sitting in her favorite booth, she indulged herself with waffles, grapefruit juice, and coffee.

Beyond the window of the diner on this summer Saturday morning, young couples were out walking dogs or pushing kids in strollers, holding tennis rackets and baseball bats, on their way to Central Park. Strolling home, Mariana smoked another cigarette—her last, she told herself. Where doormen had hosed down the pavement, it steamed.

This was the time of day she practiced. As she mounted the stairs to her apartment, she felt a rush of pure exultation. This morning, she would play on the Swan.

❧

Claude had left another message while she was out. He said he could not make contact with Baum & Fernand. The receptionist informed him that they were both away from the office that morning. What should he do? he asked. Should he come immediately to America? He could bring her back the Vuillaume and retrieve the Swan. He knew this would be "sorted out." Again, he pleaded with her to call as soon as possible.

She listened to his message several times and, by the last time, heard only the sound of his voice, not the message. Slowly, her pleasure at her lover's distress turned to confusion. He seemed so trusting, so earnest, so entirely in the dark. There must be a missing piece.

That afternoon, the phone rang and she glanced at the caller ID. It was Heinrich Baum. He invited her to meet him. "Best to talk outside the shop,"

They met at a bistro on West Fifty-fifth Street. Mariana, late as usual, arrived in a sundress and sandals, drenched in sweat. Baum, formally dressed as always, looked cool and composed. He did not smile. To steady her nerves, she ordered a mimosa. Baum was kind but stern. "I've just spoken with Roselle. What have you done with the Swan?"

She considered what to say. "What do you mean, Hanns? You know I have it."

"You're playing a dangerous game, Mariana. You cannot keep the cello. You must bring it back to me at once. I haven't told Roselle what you've done, but I will have to or he'll think it was my own mistake."

"I'll never return it."

"Don't be foolish. You can't keep it," he repeated, trying to reason with her. "Where is it?"

"I can't tell you."

"You told Roselle you picked the Swan up directly from me in a locked case."

"I did."

"What if he thinks *I* have it? That *I* was responsible? Be reasonable, Mariana."

"You can tell him whatever you want, Hanns. Tell him the truth, I don't care. I want the Swan."

"I'm sorry you're upset."

"I thought you would be on my side."

"Once upon a time, I would have been."

Mariana stared at him coldly. She picked up her bag and left the restaurant, canceling her order as she passed the waitress headed to their table bearing a mimosa on a tray.

She walked home along the border of the park. Few people were out in the intense heat. By the time she reached her apartment, dripping and out of sorts, she had decided she would leave the city and take the Swan to Stockbridge. Baum would certainly tell Claude what she'd done. But he would have to seek her out if he ever wanted to see the cello again.

Having poured herself a glass of cold water and washed her face, she went to her file cabinet and extracted the letter her father had given Beecher for her. Sitting on her couch, she reread it. Then, running the letter through her copier until the stale ink darkened, she took the clearest copy and put it an envelope addressed to Claude Roselle at his home in Lugano. Once more, she went out into the overbearing heat. She walked to the FedEx outlet and paid for the letter to reach him by overnight mail.

CHAPTER FOURTEEN

Claude

Claude returned to Lugano with the Vuillaume. On the trip home, he had controlled his agitation, but once alone in the apartment he broke down, tears of frustration on his face. He could understand nothing of what had happened or why. He felt betrayed, but by whom? Over and over, he rehearsed the moment when he opened the blue case at the bank—the crushing disappointment and the shock. Where was the Swan, *his* Swan? He could not sleep.

As soon as the office was open, Claude called Baum & Fernand. He told Baum what had happened, and the dealer gasped in disbelief. He himself, he said, had placed the Stradivarius into the case and carried it down to the taxi. There had been no mistake.

"But how could this happen? Why would she do it?" Claude asked.

"People do very strange things, I'm told, when they lose a loved one," Baum replied dryly. "Perhaps she decided that, after all, the Swan is rightfully hers."

"Rightfully *hers*? I believe it is rightfully mine."

"Since the instrument left our shop last week, we haven't seen it again. Mariana was the one who received it from us, I can assure you of that. We asked her to sign papers."

"What would make her change her mind?" He felt a chill in the nape of his neck. "Why would she want to keep the Swan from me?"

"M. Roselle," Baum answered, "as I've said, I have no idea. Could she be angry at you?"

"Absolutely not. We had a splendid visit just now in Prades." Instantly, he regretted saying this to Baum. "She flew home last night."

"Ah, I see, a weekend in Prades." The dealer paused. "Well, I am sure of one thing only, and of this I am perfectly sure. At your request, I personally handed Ms. Feldmann the Swan, in a blue fiberglass case to deliver to you."

"What do you suggest I do? I'm extremely worried."

Baum offered him no comfort. "Monsieur, I myself am not free from concern."

❧

Claude drove to Montagnola, where Francine drew him into the house. The shutters of the living room were closed against the August heat. Bernard, she said, was in Zurich and coming home that night. Claude told his mother about the missing Swan without mentioning his time with Mariana in Prades. He said they'd met only briefly in Barcelona so she could give him the cello.

"I *wish* you'd told me about your arrangements." His mother's face was flushed. "I've said repeatedly that Mariana is a troubled woman and not to be trusted. Is she still in Europe? Have you demanded an explanation?"

"I can't reach her," Claude admitted. "Nobody knows where she is."

"No one? Who have you asked?"

He paced. "I called Heinrich Baum, of course. And he had no idea what happened. He swore he himself put the Swan in its case and handed it to Mariana."

"We must call the police!"

"No, Maman, not yet."

"God only knows what she's done with the Swan. Or what she's planning to do. Perhaps they're conspiring, she and Baum." Francine fanned herself. She seemed about to faint.

"Calm down, Maman. She hasn't been given a chance to explain. I'm not ready to contact the authorities yet. This is a misunderstanding, I'm sure."

"Don't be a fool."

They shared an angry silence. He did not stay for lunch.

❧

When Claude returned to his apartment, he found a FedEx envelope wedged against the door. He tossed it onto the piano and went to check his answering machine. There were no messages. Again, he called Mariana and did not reach her. Returning to the living room, he considered booking a flight to New York. But what good would that do? He had no idea where she was. Baffled, he picked up the FedEx envelope. He saw it was from Mariana and felt excitement and relief. Here, surely, was the answer to the mystery.

He tore it open. Inside was a single photocopied sheet, with Alexander Feldmann's name and address at the top. Claude, holding the letter, recognized his mentor's beautiful script. The letter was addressed to Mariana. "As I'm sure you have known and been much affected by, your mother and I were not happy together..."

The signature at the bottom was his teacher's. Claude reread the letter, feeling sick. Alexander Feldmann, his great hero, had been sleeping with his mother, traveling with her, for all these years. Not years, decades. This was the man he had revered. And his mother—the deceit and disloyalty were staggering. Did people know? Had she exposed his father, Bernard, to ridicule?

To a small boy, Alexander had been larger than life, sweeping in, dashing out on his way to one engagement or another, playful and subversive in a way that made Claude feel important and grown up. "We men," Feldmann would say, "will now have a cello lesson." Francine, beaming, would leave them alone together. "We men will take a walk, we men will watch some tennis..." Alexander would sit on the couch with his arm around Claude, practicing fingerings on his shoulder as they watched Pete Sampras serve. He tousled Claude's hair, slapped his knee companionably, and when there was an exciting shot, squeezed his cheeks or kissed him. It was all so breathtakingly un-Swiss.

The lessons, too, inspired the boy. He wanted not only to follow in Alexander's footsteps but to literally *become* him. It was not that he didn't love his own father, but Bernard seemed—by comparison—dull and remote. Alexander knew no boundaries; he was everywhere at once, noisy and dominant, full of life.

Over time, however, his relationship with Alexander changed. The more seriously his teacher took his playing, the less playful he became. Instead, the maestro grew more demanding and impatient. He criticized, he mocked, he pushed. He could be ruthlessly tactless. Lessons were long, but when they were over Feldmann put them immediately behind him. "Well, my boy, let's have a game of chess." If Claude showed signs of frustration or resentment, Alexander would explain, "I only criticize you this way because I admire your talent. I think you could be great someday. I believe in you."

❧

Holding the letter, Claude paced the living room. Of course he had long realized that his parents had an unusual marriage, so often apart, so independent. He had simply believed this was the natural result of their culture and of their great commitment to music. To think his cello lessons had been merely a pretext for his mother's trysts with Alexander! Francine's eagerness to keep him at the instrument had probably been a ruse, a way to cover up her affair. To think he had been so sure that he himself was the center of his mother's world, that Feldmann came all the way from America to supervise his protégé because of Claude's blazing talent.

Trembling, he looked at the date of the letter; oh, God—Mariana had known all along, since their meeting in Boston. He remembered Edith Libbey's telling him that his mother had often visited her with Feldmann; the secretary had said Francine preferred this painting or that. He remembered too the look that night in Mariana's eyes. She knew. Everywhere he traveled in America, people knew his mother and her connection to the great cellist. In Europe, too, there must have been rumors. It hurt Claude to think Bernard might have known all along and accepted his wife's adultery for fear of losing her or — worse yet, perhaps — of losing face in his conservative milieu.

He hadn't been suspicious of his mother's grief when Alexander died. How tenderly he had comforted her and admired the depth of her capacity for friendship, how completely she had fooled him! Would she have left her husband and son had Alexander made an offer? Would she have run to him? Had she waited all these decades, hoping they would one day merge their lives? Did Alexander dash those hopes over and over again?

As far as he himself was concerned, Mariana could have the fucking Swan. He wanted no part of it now. No part of Alexander Feldmann or his mother or the Silver Swan, no part of love affairs or marriage — just his career, his music, and random sexual encounters when opportunity arose. He was furious. He sat down at the counter, staring at nothing. But after a while, he stood up again. Steadying himself, he reconsidered. He thought he might still change his mind about this impulse to give up the Swan. It was, after all, the most magnificent of instruments and it *was* his.

⁂

That night, depressed and shaken, Claude went to dine with Sophie. He told her he would not marry her. He would support their child and try to be the best father he could be, but he was unfit to be a husband. He was, he said, drinking his third glass of wine, an emotional disaster.

"An emotional disaster," Sophie repeated. "What does that mean?" She looked at him in perfect incomprehension. Yet she seemed to understand he was being sincere, because he never before had spoken to her so openly about his feelings. Over espresso he told her he intended to take a break, a short trip.

She listened, looking down. "Do you go with Mariana?"

"No, Sophie, alone."

Why did women always think the problem was another woman? Even when they were correct, it was irritating. "It's everything," he answered. "I no longer am able to believe what I've always believed, to think what I've always thought. Can you understand this, Sophie?"

Now she raised her eyes to his. "It is very difficult."

⁂

The next morning, he woke to the telephone's ring; it was early and the night before he'd had far too much to drink. Head throbbing, he reached for the phone.

"Claude? I've been trying to reach you, *chéri*." His mother was breathless. "I couldn't sleep all night. If you haven't heard from Mariana, I think we really must call Interpol."

He swallowed. His ears were ringing, his mouth was dry. "No."

"Do you have a better idea?"

"I don't think you'll want me to call anyone"—his voice was hoarse—"when you hear what I'm going to say."

"Excuse me?"

"Feldmann wrote his daughter a letter about you and your long affair. At least you will be gratified to know he called you his great love, even if he never wanted more from you than occasional pleasure." Claude was caustic. "He wrote this letter before he died. She has sent me a copy. In her fragile state, she might be tempted to show it to Papa, which you would not like, would you? Unless, that is, you've already told Papa about your affair with Alexander Feldmann?"

"I don't understand you, Claude. Are you drunk? What are you talking about?"

Bitterly, he told her of the FedEx delivery and read her Alexander's letter, sparing her nothing. Francine was silent.

"What have you to say for yourself?" Claude asked.

"Claude," Francine said at last, "please let us talk about this. Don't be harsh." He heard her beginning to cry. "We were very much in love, *chéri*. It was not trivial. In the end, he came back to ask me to marry him, and I said no, I would never leave you and your father."

"I don't care. I don't want to hear about it."

"It was wrong of Mariana to tell you."

His tongue felt hard and thick. He was parched. "Mariana has turned against me. We'd been becoming friends, even though she knew all this, and now she wants the Strad."

"You're being unfair, Claude. You can't understand, and of course you're upset. Perhaps I do owe you an explanation—but you mustn't lose the Swan. Not just because you're angry with me. It's so important to your career—"

He cut her off. "My career is not your business. Not any longer. Feldmann is dead. You can retire."

"Did he say anything else in this letter to Mariana?"

"Wasn't that enough?"

"Mariana has wronged us all."

"No, Maman, you have."

Claude rose from his bed, holding his phone to his ear, and went to the bathroom to pour himself a glass of water. "I do have one question to ask you, and you had better tell me the truth. What did you tell Mariana when she called you several weeks ago, looking for me? Did you say anything about Sophie, about her pregnancy?"

It took Francine a moment to answer. "I did, Claude. I thought it was the right thing to do—because I thought you would do the right thing for Sophie."

"What did you *tell* her?" he roared. He would have shaken her had they been in the same room.

"I told her you were getting married."

This too took his breath away. Claude was aghast. "But I'm not. I'm not getting married to Sophie."

"Oh, but you must. She's carrying your child!"

"I'm not in love with her. Our marriage would be like yours. Would you want that for me?" It gave Claude great satisfaction to say this. "You should know that I *am* in love with Mariana." In the ensuing silence, he wondered if this were true.

"You're not acting honorably," Francine said, sobbing.

"Look in the mirror, Madame." He slammed the telephone down.

CHAPTER FIFTEEN

Mariana

The morning after she sent the letter, Mariana packed up, put the Silver Swan in the Vuillaume's empty case, and drove to Stockbridge. She stopped in town to buy groceries at the Public Market and gin at Good Wines and Spirits. At Swann's Way, the borders of the rutted driveway were overgrown, the flower beds a wild tangle of weeds and vines and drooping blooms. She got out of the car and, carrying the cello, let herself into the airless house. As she opened windows, clustered dust balls blew along the floor.

She took the Silver Swan out of the case and carried it to the safe, where she hung it on the last remaining strap, next to all its imitators. She closed the heavy door. Only her Vuillaume was absent. She missed it, despite the presence of the original.

The dining room table wore a layer of dust, as did the marble-topped sideboard. The chandelier was swathed in cobwebs. Opening the French doors that gave out onto the terrace, where at night she could watch the purple fading light as the moon rose over the mountains, she felt Claude's presence everywhere. She wished he would step from the garden's edge into her arms. How could she have thought he might love her? What was he thinking now? How would he feel when he read Alexander's letter? Would he reproach himself for lying to her about Sophie von Whatever?

The drive had tired her. She went back to Alexander's studio and closed the doors. Settling on the suede couch where her father had taken his afternoon naps, she kicked off her shoes. His plaid mohair throw blanket hung over the arm of the couch, folded. Her mother had made it. Mariana pulled it around her shoulders and lay down, enveloped by memories of her mother at work with her crochet hook and knitting needles in the living room while her father gave lessons.

This Mariana had understood: no one could make the music Alexander made without drawing from a well of sensitivity and emotional intelligence. In his last years, because he had shared his time so generously, students and colleagues came back to visit or play for him, to take lessons or make movies, to tape or talk to him about music. So many asked to come that visits had to be carefully scheduled so as not to exhaust him. As he joked with Mariana, "They come to touch the hem of my robe."

Even such devotion failed to compensate Alexander for the loss of his strength and agility on the instrument—the daily diminution of prowess. He practiced every morning and grew frustrated and then pained by the sound he produced, by how quickly he tired, how everything hurt. And, in his late eighties, when his eyesight, like his mother's, began to fail, he could play only what he remembered, often stopping in the middle of a passage. The look of despair and confusion on his face at those moments so distressed Mariana that she would rush to him to hum the rest of the phrase or go to the piano to play it. Together, they would work their way through music he once knew by heart.

One day, while in the kitchen making lunch for Alexander, she heard him stop playing abruptly. When he didn't come to the dining room, she went to see if something had happened—or what the distraction had been. Entering his studio, she saw that he was sitting with the cello, head resting against the fingerboard, eyes closed. Tears streamed down his old face. "I can't, Mariana, I can't go on without my music. I can't see anymore, I can barely lift my arms. It's not possible." She had gone to stand behind him, stroking his shoulders. "No use," he kept saying. "No use."

As he declined into helplessness, the reverence she had always felt for him was no longer tempered by fear. Now she could tell him she loved him, knowing, even though he did not say it, that he felt love for her too. She sat with her father as he slept, reading in a rocking chair beside his bed. With his head nestled on his favorite old pillow, he would move the fingers of his left hand on his cheek, playing, always playing his cello. His dreams were often violent and frightening. He would wake up, terror in his lined face, and look at Mariana until he understood who she was. Then he would reach for her hand and sigh. "This is no longer useful," he would say, "this life I'm living—no use to it, sweetheart."

⁂

That night, she dined alone, listening to NPR and treating herself to a good bottle of Bordeaux from Alexander's excellent cellar. She had come to settle his affairs. Over dinner, she made lists of all the tasks ahead. The next morning, she went to work. Sitting on the floor of Alexander's studio, she opened the first carton of his papers and began to sort. There were reviews and testimonials and accolades, letters of gratitude from students, contracts and royalty statements and programs and posters—a paper monument to Alexander's eminence and to his self-love. He had saved everything, bringing home every last bit of evidence from all over the world that his career was a success, that he was idolized. Pilar had not organized these documents by category or year; she had simply thrown them in boxes. When a box was full, she taped it up and stacked it on the studio shelves, with not so much as a date. To Mariana, this represented her mother's small rebellion against the tyranny of Alexander's self-importance.

Interspersed among the yellowed newspaper clippings and photographs dating back to Alexander's days at Juilliard, Mariana found the deed to Swann's Way, contracts with those luthiers who had fashioned copies of the Stradivarius, tax statements, bills of sale, and her own birth certificate. She realized she would have to go through every sheet in these mountains of paper or risk throwing out documents she would need in the future. Working her way through box after box, slicing the brittle tape, she sifted and read. Hour after hour, her anger mounted at the sheer disorder of his so-called legacy. If he cared so much, why had he not hired someone to organize it?

Once in a while, she found a personal letter. These she read carefully. The bulk of them were dull. A few—such as the letters from Zena Padrova—were witty and charming. But there was a common theme to all the correspondence—everybody flattered Feldmann, everyone wanted his help. Perhaps, she thought, he had actually discarded anything less than flattering.

Slowly, it grew clear to Mariana that she was hunting for something—a shard of evidence, however small in this accumulation of an entire life, that she herself existed—something he might have written about her or saved: a letter or a school report card, or even a program from one of her own concerts. Between that tattered certificate marking her birth and the letter she'd received in Boston upon his death, apparently Alexander had deemed nothing about her important enough to save among his papers. Absolutely nothing.

Mariana closed her eyes. She rolled her shoulders and neck. She could refuse to be consumed by Alexander's earthly afterlife, she told herself, as she had been by the man while alive.

⁂

Days later, as she approached the end of her task, sorting through one of the few remaining boxes, she found a large sheaf of documents from Alexander's concert management, dated 1983. While she was flipping through the stapled contracts, an envelope fluttered to her lap. It had been sent to her father care of the office and was marked on the outside: "Please deliver to Mr. Feldmann. Confidential." The envelope had been opened. Mariana withdrew the letter, handwritten on onionskin grown fragile with age.

September 12, 1980

My dearest A,

I hope it will not be too long before you receive my letter; I have sent it via your concert management. I assume they will give it to you promptly, as I know you are now at home. I wanted you to know that I shall be coming to New York with Bernard and

Claude in ten days and, even with all these constraints, it would be good to see you, if only for a short visit. The Kappelmans know I am coming and will, of course, offer us some protection for one or two encounters alone.

I have missed you terribly and I am so eager to have you spend some time with Claude; at five, he is becoming such a darling miniature of his father. He will not be as tall, perhaps, but he has your beautiful hands and, above all, he has your talent. It is emerging in a way that will please and gratify and even amuse you. But he will need your time and attention, not only for his development on the cello, but because it is only right that he know you. If the only capacity in which he can know you is as teacher, and if he never knows the truth of our relationship, this will at least give him something of you. Should he ever find out, he will at least feel you have cared for him and participated in raising him.

Long ago you told me that I might dream of a time when you and I could be together as man and wife to raise our son. I have held on to that dream, and my desire to spend my life with you has not lessened over time, even as my hopes have diminished. Shall I see you in New York?

Je t'aime,

Francine

Stricken, Mariana dropped the letter, and into the late afternoon silence she screamed, "God damn you, god damn you, Alexander Feldmann," into the empty room. She stood up abruptly and pulled a large photo of Alexander from the wall, held it over her head, and dashed it to the floor. Glass fractured and splintered, the frame shattered against the wall.

As a result of his unfathomable selfishness, she had fallen in love—she was having an affair—with her own half brother. How callously evil it was for her father to bring them together after his death, with no thought of the consequences, no impulse to warn them, to be honest, to come clean. Claude was Alexander's son, Mariana his daughter. Their father had known this but had refused to acknowledge the truth of it. Even in death, he had kept his silence and deprived her of the chance for happiness.

Claude would have to know the truth. She would not bear this secret alone, nor would she spare his mother the confrontation that would surely ensue.

❦

For several days, Mariana could not bring herself to eat, to practice, to leave the house or resume her grim task. She moved from room to room, from bed to couch to bed, suffering, trying to sleep, waiting for the phone to ring, to hear Claude's voice. He didn't call. Finally she drove into Stockbridge and FedExed a copy of Francine's letter to him in Lugano.

She had no one. Her mother and father were dead. Anton had returned to his family. Claude would marry Sophie. Her friendships had suffered neglect in the years since she'd left New York to tend to Alexander. She could not confide in her few acquaintances in Stockbridge and Tanglewood. They were hardly friends.

Finally, when Claude did not call, she went back to work, but this time with a different purpose. Plugging in the paper shredder Alexander had kept under his desk and never used, she began to feed paper into its grinding teeth. Each time the shredder bin grew full, she emptied it into a large green garbage bag. She drank coffee to stay awake. In her nightgown, her long, aching legs stretched in front of her, she flung the empty boxes into the foyer where they piled up, strewn like giant building blocks. The dark green bags formed a separate, growing mound.

When she had stripped Alexander's studio, she carried the trash bags to the kitchen porch. She moved the empty boxes there as well. After her orgy of shredding, Alexander's legacy was reduced to his recordings and his collection of music manuscripts, marked with his fingerings and bowings and commentary that might interest future cellists. These she would give to the Juilliard library.

One early morning, when the shelves and closets and walls were at last empty, she turned off the security alarm and strode out into the garden behind the house. Faint light on the eastern horizon lit her way. She approached the unused swimming pool at the back of the garden and, with effort, turned the rusty crank that rolled up its ancient canvas cover. The empty pool, its pale green paint cracked and strewn with leaves, glowed eerily in the half-light.

Crossing back and forth from kitchen porch to pool, Mariana tossed box after box into the waterless hole. In the silent dawn, the dull thud of the falling boxes reverberated like blows. Then she emptied the garbage bags, flapping them over the boxes, a snowstorm of fluttery strips. A slight breeze blew from the west.

She carried the empty garbage bags back to the kitchen. On the counter, her cell phone blinked. She had a message. She put the phone in the pocket of the old sweater she'd thrown over her nightgown. Picking up the box of long matches by the fireplace and a piece of newspaper, she headed back into the garden. At the pool's edge she rolled up the newspaper, struck a match, and set it alight. She tossed it onto the shredded paper pile.

Flames flew up instantly, brilliantly, into the sky. Mariana, retreating, walked backward toward the kitchen, watching the growing fire. Burning wisps of Alexander's legacy floated up like fireflies, then fireworks. They drifted over the garden and toward the house, rising and falling in the light breeze.

She stepped inside and watched the conflagration through the kitchen windows. Minutes passed as she stared, transfixed. Oh, Alexander—all that self-love, all that history she'd set aflame, was burning and turning to ash.

Pressing her face against the window, she suddenly noticed that the fire was spreading beyond the pool, leaping toward the house, carried by wisps of burning paper. Pilar's large baskets of pinecones erupted in flame. Fire licked at the white posts of the porch. Smoke curled toward the windows and through the open kitchen door. Horrified, she pulled her cell phone from her pocket and called 911. Flames inched, then jumped, then raced along the porch. The noise was loud, the kitchen too was beginning to burn.

Running down the hall to Alexander's studio, she felt the heat advancing at her back. Her hands shook as she removed the paintings, pushed aside the false wall, and tried to open the safe. Several times, in the dim light, she failed to enter the right combination. When at last she succeeded, she pulled open the heavy door and reached for the Swan, grateful she'd hung it on the last hook, easily found. She pulled it off the loop and pushed the door closed. Fleeing the studio, she crossed the foyer to the front door and wrenched it open.

At the end of the corridor behind her, she saw fire. Mariana turned and, clutching the instrument, ran toward the front door. In her terrified haste—trying to remember what they said to do in fire, to stay low and not breathe deeply—she bumped the cello hard against the doorframe. There was a loud popping sound.

Mariana staggered down the front steps, clutching the Swan, and bolted from the house. Safely away, she ran her hands over the Swan and felt an opened seam down the middle of its back. Weeping with remorse, she awaited the fire trucks. There were sirens in the distance. She could hear them first, and then trucks rumbling up the driveway. Through the trees, Mariana saw the flashing strobes of light.

CHAPTER SIXTEEN

Claude and Mariana

The kitchen addition had burned to the ground, but the main house suffered only smoke damage. In that regard, she was lucky. The cellos left in the vault had fared better than the Stradivarius she'd tried to save. The Swan now had a crack along its back, where it had hit the doorframe as she rushed from the house.

Mariana, staying at the Red Lion Inn, was finally able to check her cell phone for messages. She had dropped it in the grass as she fled the house three days earlier, and the insurance inspector found and returned it. There was only one message. Claude had left it on the day of the fire.

"Mariana, dear Mariana, won't you pick up the phone? Won't you call me, please? I must speak with you; there has been a terrible misunderstanding. If you'll agree to meet me, I'll come back to America immediately. My mother told you that I planned to marry Sophie, and I can imagine how much this hurt. But darling, it's not true. How could you have believed her? It was a misunderstanding on her part. She only hoped I *would* marry Sophie, for reasons I'll explain when we meet. I beg you to call me."

Mariana suspected he had not yet received her second FedEx when he left this message. By now he would have it. She dialed his number.

"It's Mariana," she said when he answered the phone.

"Where are you?"

"At the Red Lion Inn in Stockbridge. I set the house on fire. I didn't mean to. It was an accident."

"Are you hurt?"

"No."

"Thank God."

"But the Swan suffered some damage."

He froze. After a moment, he said, "So have we all, so have we all."

Mariana did not answer.

"I've read the letter you found in your father's papers. I haven't spoken with my mother since then, but she sent me a letter as well. I'd like to read it to you."

"I'm not sure I want to hear it, Claude."

"Mariana. We have no more secrets. Please listen." He read:

> "Dear Claude:
>
> "You know now of my long love affair with Alexander Feldmann. Here is the last piece of the story; I will be direct. You are Feldmann's child. Perhaps you felt you had a special kinship with him and were not entirely astonished when the Stradivarius that was his great treasure became yours.
>
> "Papa does not know. I have managed for thirty-five years to keep my secret from him and from you. You must try to understand how much it would hurt him to know. Perhaps you will find a way to forgive me for what you will think of as betrayal.

Maybe we can talk honestly at some moment in the future when conversation is again possible. This is why you do deserve the cello; it comes from someone who loved you and knew you were his son.

"I remain, as always, your entirely devoted and loving

"Maman"

&

Two weeks later, after Claude had played his last concert of the summer season, he and Mariana met in New York. At seven thirty on a Tuesday night, Claude sat at Cafe Luxembourg awaiting her. He'd asked the maître d' for the table they had dined at in April. Leaning back and drumming his fingers nervously on his leg, he drank a double Macallan, neat. Ten minutes passed. He practiced phrases while he watched the entrance for Mariana's arrival. On his flight to Kennedy, he had tried to imagine this moment, so much hanging in the balance.

It would not be simple. She too would need a drink. He wondered if he should order for her or choose a fine bottle of wine. On the plane he had sat beside the J.-B. Vuillaume in its bright blue case. Claude had not touched it for all the weeks it stood in his hall closet. It belonged to Mariana. But he had resolved to his personal satisfaction his own conflict about the Stradivarius. Since he was Alexander's son, he was, one could say, as much an heir to the great instrument as Mariana. He was almost certain they could come to an agreement.

The restaurant was filling up. He felt conspicuously alone. He wanted another scotch but decided to wait till she joined him. One thing he'd begun to understand about her—she had an elastic sense of time. She well might be an hour too early or late. "Punctuality," his father liked to say, "is the politeness of kings." But not necessarily of queens! Claude thought.

As if on cue, however, she appeared in the restaurant's entrance. The maître d' led her to his table. Mariana hurried toward him. Sharply, he drew in his breath; she was astonishing—tan, tall, and slender, long arms and legs bare despite the evening's chill. She wore a short black sheath, anchored on one shoulder. Her thick, dark hair fell in wild curls and her eyes were lined in black pencil. She had lost weight, perhaps a bit too much. How, he wondered, should he greet her? Would they kiss on the lips?

In the European manner, she leaned forward to brush both his cheeks. "I thought this moment would never arrive." She was breathless. Dropping her shawl on the table, she sat. Her eyes filled with tears as she searched his face. "I've missed you."

He reached out his hand. She did not take it. "I've been wretched. And a wretch as well. I don't know what possessed me to take the Swan from you."

The waiter approached. Claude ordered a second Macallan—a single, this time—and she requested a kir.

"You were very angry when you thought I'd marry Sophie."

Mariana half smiled, rueful. "Yes, I was. Such a history of anger. First, I was angry at my father for his affair with your mother. Then I was angry at him for giving you the Swan, then angry at you for accepting the gift, and then enraged that you were to marry Sophie. And then the shattering discovery that we share a father..."

He started to tell her that he understood, but she put up her hand to stop him.

"Please, Claude. I'm trying to apologize. I need to set this whole business straight. You must have been furious, outraged when you opened the cello case in Barcelona."

He didn't answer. She was silent as their drinks arrived.

"I've been unable," Mariana continued, "to eat or sleep. I've been scared you would never forgive me for what's happened to the Swan. I had almost made peace with my father's decision to give it to you. You and the cello together were part of my future, my life. I felt almost fortunate, Claude, that it worked out this way, that you would own the instrument"—she paused and looked into his eyes—"because when I met you I fell in love with you."

Trembling, he shifted in his chair. What *had* happened to the Swan? He desperately wanted to ask, but she had just told him she was in love with him. He would have to wait.

"Your mother lied to me about Sophie and I believed her. I believed her because in my experience, men were more than capable of such treachery. It was dangerous to want you so much."

She was using the past tense, he noticed. Was she no longer in love with him?

"I remember when you said, 'Mariana, too many times you've been left by a cellist.' When you went away, I suddenly realized you meant that you too would be leaving me. I was crushed." She paused. "Do you also remember you told me we could never be separated—the Swan would be our bond? I believed you. But after I spoke with your mother—"

"I know, I *know*," he interrupted, slightly impatient. "She wasn't exactly lying. She actually thought I'd marry Sophie because Sophie is pregnant. She just assumed I'd marry the mother of my child because she believed it the right thing to do."

Mariana drew back, stricken. "She's pregnant? Sophie is pregnant? It's *your* baby? Did you know?"

"Not until I got home. Till after I left you."

"And"—she swallowed—"you won't marry her?"

"I can't." He felt accused.

"You're a father," she said sadly. "You'll *be* a father, anyhow."

"Yes, I will. But not a husband. I am fond of Sophie but I don't love her. She will be happier with someone who does."

She looked away. Her earrings were burnished gold loops; her necklace too was gold.

He could smell her perfume, familiar and arousing. He felt as if he were caught in one of those dreams where the goal was close, whatever it was, and yet it kept receding. One couldn't reach it. He wanted to ask about the Swan, to find out what had happened to it. Waiting for the right moment, he could hardly hear what she said. She went in and out of focus while they ordered dinner and the food arrived.

Finally she said, "Claude, I put the Swan at risk. We almost lost it."

He flushed. "What happened? Where is it?"

"I took the Swan to Stockbridge to keep it away from you. When I was running from the burning house, I knocked it against the door. I only wanted to save it, but it was difficult to see, for all the smoke... There's been some damage. If only I'd just left it in the safe with the other cellos, it wouldn't have the back crack it has now."

Claude felt dizzy. His hands trembled. The instrument had been in terrible danger. It was gravely damaged. He remembered his mother's warning—Mariana could be wild and self-destructive. Was it possible she had destroyed the Swan? A back crack could ruin an instrument.

After a moment he was able to ask, "How serious is the crack? You must tell me. Have you contacted Pierre Fernand? Has he looked at it?"

Mariana studied his face, drawing back into her chair. "Yes, I've contacted him. He's back at the shop. And no, he has not seen it. He is very angry with me. He and Baum, both. I've promised to take it to the shop tomorrow night."

"But surely people must know," he persisted.

"I think not yet." Her tone was cooler. "I've spoken to no one and no one yet knows the Swan was there with me. But it will come out."

Again Claude drank. He had to get control of himself and the intense anger he felt. He was silent for a while. "If news of this gets out, the Swan will lose half its value. Maybe more, depending on the extent of the damage."

"We have to hope the extent of the damage won't be public... but that's unlikely. I *myself* only care that it can be restored."

"It may not have the same sound." He was reproachful. "This can happen, as you know, with a back crack."

"I know." She looked down. "My father would never forgive me."

"*Our* father would never forgive you," he corrected her, "but he's *dead* and it's our problem. We'll have to wait until Fernand examines it."

She felt a flash of anger and mistrust. Perhaps he thought he had disguised his largest concern — the fate of the Swan — but he had not kept it from her. Like Alexander, she thought, he did not have that kind of subtlety. She stood up abruptly and excused herself. In the ladies' room, she pressed her forehead with a damp paper towel. She had allowed herself to think that the Swan's fate would not be his first concern—that he would be heartbroken by the discovery they shared a father and their affair was incestuous. But, for him, the Swan came first, and *that* was disturbingly familiar.

Claude thought she might be walking out of the restaurant and half rose from his seat to follow her, but he froze with indecision, unable to choose between colliding impulses. He wanted her; he wanted to capture and restore the deep twinned bonds of desire and music they had so easily formed. But in that moment, he also wanted to take the cello and return to the world he had inhabited before they met.

When Mariana turned away from the door and toward the ladies' room, Claude sank back into his chair. Then he took up his drink and considered the fate of the cello, what he would do if it were irreparably damaged.

Mariana returned to the table, composed and remote. "I'll go home now, Claude. We'll meet to take the cello to Baum & Fernand tomorrow. Now I'm too tired to eat."

"I'll take you in a taxi," he offered.

"No, thank you. I'll walk."

"Shall I walk with you?"

"No. No, thanks. I don't want company."

As they waited for the check, Claude pressed her. "I've brought back your Vuillaume. I want you to play it for me."

"I haven't practiced for quite a while."

"Of course you haven't. I've had your cello."

"And Baum now has the other copies." She paused. "I'm not sure I want to play for you."

"Please, it would mean so much to me. Think about it for a day."

"How long will you be here?"

"I've three days."

As they parted, Claude embraced her. She pulled back and said good night.

❧

Mariana walked north along Central Park West toward home. It was late and dark. A breeze made the awnings of the buildings luff pleasantly, and doormen loitered under the lighted canopies in the fresh night air. Trapped in a vortex of feelings, she could at first make no sense of what had happened at the restaurant. She had gone to meet Claude to apologize for her deceit in Barcelona and the damage she'd inflicted on the cello. She wanted to beg his forgiveness and hoped he would come home with her at the evening's end to take her to bed. She wanted to tell him she loved him and didn't care about the past, their shared father, the Swan—about anything but their love affair and its future. But as the evening continued, she grew to understand this could never be. He did not want what she wanted. He had not returned to *her*, he had come back to claim the Swan. Claude was his father's son. He was no less charming, no less serious a musician, if not possessed of an equivalent talent. His sweetness had misled her, but he was equally unavailable and ill equipped to love. She wondered if Claude, in time, would become another Alexander, always seeking further recognition of his talent and further affirmation that his public revered him and his precious gift.

Mariana had a restless night. She was furious with Claude, but even more so with herself. She knew she would have to master the great attraction she felt for him. It would bring her no happiness. Nonetheless, and despite her disappointment and anger, she would have to come to terms with her half brother. He was her only living relative, and he owned the Swan.

CHAPTER SEVENTEEN

Mariana and Claude

Claude called from his hotel the next morning. He offered to bring her the Vuillaume. She invited him to her apartment and greeted him barefoot, dressed in jeans and a white T-shirt. He handed her a bouquet of freesia, a bag of pastries, and the cello in its bright blue case.

"If you don't mind, now while I'm here," he said, "I'll practice on your Vuillaume to keep my hands in shape."

"That would be fine. I won't mind at all. But I won't play for you just yet. I'm not ready."

He kissed her cheek. "How are you? You left so abruptly last night."

Mariana took the flowers and went to find a vase. Claude walked around her living room, looking at the art on the walls and the photographs. It was, he said, a charming place. She wondered how long he could wait to ask to see the Swan. They sat by the bay window, drinking coffee and eating the pastries Claude had brought. Finishing, he said, "I must see the Swan, hard as it will be. I know you don't want me to."

It didn't take him long to ask, she thought. She went to her bedroom, opened the closet, and laid the Swan upon her bed, with its back against the covers. Then she invited Claude to come in and left him with the instrument, unwilling to witness his first shock. When she returned, she found him sitting with the Swan across his knees. He was running his fingers along the crack, back and forth, caressing it as though it were a dying animal; tears streamed down his face. Mariana took the Swan from him and, putting it down, embraced him with renewed tenderness. He loved the Swan, as she did. Over and over again, she whispered, "I'm sorry. I'm so sorry."

"The Swan hasn't made anyone happy," Claude murmured. "Except Alexander."

"Strange, isn't it, how much trouble it's caused."

"Starting with — or so I heard — the sacrifices you and your mother made to pay for it."

"No. Starting with the fact that your mother and my father met when he went to Strasbourg to find it."

"Our father," he reminded her.

"And then you and I met in Boston." Mariana sighed. "The Swan has brought us together. Let's not allow it to break us apart." She took the cello from him and returned it to its case. It was time to tell him about the offer from the Metropolitan Museum.

❧

They spent the day together, wandering the city and talking. Riding the ferry to Staten Island and back, she pointed out the space where the World Trade Center once stood. "This happened when I was with Anton in Europe."

"Are you in touch with Pietovsky?"

"He sent a sweet condolence note when Alexander died. But, no, we're not in touch."

They walked along the Hudson in Riverside Park on their way back to her apartment. The wind was strong and the clouds sped swiftly by, creating flashes of light, then shadow. "Claude, there's something else I should tell you," she said. "After I returned from Prades, I was approached by the curator of the Mertens Collection."

"What's that? I'm not familiar with it."

"The Metropolitan Museum of Art's rare instrument collection. It's very great. The curator's name is Andrew Macintosh, a Scotsman. I met him a while back. My father gave a private concert for some major donors years ago, and Macintosh suggested I might want to consider making a gift of the Silver Swan to the Met. He knew I wasn't concertizing anymore. He believed Alexander had 'a special relationship' to the museum. He didn't understand, of course, that the Swan wasn't mine to give..."

A boy on a skateboard raced past. Another followed, wobbling.

"*Did* Alexander have such a special relationship?" Claude asked.

"No," she answered, laughing. "He played at Grace Rainey Rogers many times, but to him, I suspect, it was just another concert hall. He wasn't much interested in museums, as I've told you. 'Special relationship'—it's the kind of thing people say to encourage generosity."

"*My* generosity, I suppose it would have to be now."

"The Swan is yours, and yours to dispose of as you see fit. But I thought I should mention it anyhow, given the crack."

He stopped and turned to face her. "Why do you think I should make a gift of it to a museum?"

"We have to think about what to do if the Swan fails to regain its beauty of tone—if Fernand can't make it sing again. It might be wise to consider the offer. The dealers will know it's been repaired. This offer from the Mertens Collection might be the best we can do."

"Presuming I do want to give up ownership."

"Presuming you do, yes." She adjusted her sunglasses, nodding. The river smelled dank. She could tell he was not ready to relinquish what he'd not yet possessed. "Claude, I'm trying to be helpful, realistic. Of course all decisions are yours to make."

"Don't you remember," he protested, "Alexander always railed against putting great instruments away, locking them up in glass boxes in museums?"

"Like most other institutions, they would be willing—after a brief exhibition—to loan it back to you. It's often a condition of the gift: you play it for your lifetime. But when your career is over, it returns to the Met, permanently, unless they want to loan it out again."

"Do they suggest I simply give it to them as a gift?"

"No, of course not an outright gift. The curator assured me that between the tax advantages of a donation and a pledge he's received from a donor, they could make a handsome offer. Not market price, but substantial."

"What did they offer?"

"They didn't make a firm offer. That they must make to you, not me. I put them off. But after the repairs I'm sure we would still have a great deal of money."

Puzzled, he said, "*We?*"

It was time, she knew, to speak of this. "I don't mean I expect to get anything like half. I do realize Alexander left you the Swan. But if you thought it were fair, I'd like to have enough to allow me to keep Swann's Way and pay the taxes on the rest of the estate."

Frowning, he looked out over the Hudson. "Do the dealers know yet what happened? To the Strad, I mean."

"Not as far as I know. But these things are hard to keep secret in the music world. The fire in Stockbridge was certainly not reported in New York, though most of the Tanglewood crowd heard about it. The fire, that is, not the cello."

"And what if it *does* retain its sound? It would be worth far more than any museum would pay."

"Why don't we wait and see," she suggested.

❧

At eight o'clock that evening, Mariana and Claude met Pierre Fernand at his office. They brought the Swan. Pierre had made a special arrangement to come and receive them, though he was not yet regularly back at work. He looked frail and walked with a slight limp. The showroom was dark. They went straight back to his workshop. Heinrich Baum was traveling, he told them, inviting them to sit on the high stools grouped at his table.

Mariana fingered a scroll. It was unvarnished, "in the white."

"Pierre," she began, "I've had an unfortunate accident with the Swan."

"So I have heard," he answered. She and Claude were startled.

"Yes, of course we have heard about that terrible fire. Almost a tragedy." He paused. "But the copies were saved, in the safe, and the Swan, she has some damage, but she does not burn. *Oui?* Baum talked with somebody at Tanglewood."

Mariana and Claude exchanged glances. She said, "I'm afraid it has a crack. On the back, near the sound post and easy to see. We've come to ask if you would take a look at it and tell us what you think—how much work it would require and what you would charge for repairs."

He faced her squarely. "I am disappointed in you, Mariana. First you run away with the Swan and then you put it near a fire and give it a bonk. Your poor *papa.* Imagine he is turning in his grave. You have not treated it with respect, and now look what has happened. I am sad for M. Roselle to have this trouble—and for your father." He sighed. "But we will take a look."

Pierre opened the case and laid the Swan gently on his worktable under the hanging light. As he turned it over, he winced. The cello was badly wounded. He said nothing for a while but continued to inspect the maple with great tenderness. Watching, Mariana felt nothing but shame.

"What can I tell you?" he said at last. "This is, *hélas*, a big bit of damage. I can repair it, yes, but I guarantee only the way she will look. And it takes months, not weeks."

"When can you begin?" Claude asked.

"I must open her up, as you know. It will not be easy or cheap. There will be papers to sign. M. Roselle will be willing?"

"Yes," he answered, "we are in complete agreement."

"Good. I would like to see the crack from inside. I will open her up? Together we will assess her damage, if you like."

"Yes, of course," Claude said again, but Mariana said nothing. Pierre removed the strings and—because the tension of the strings no longer held it in place, he lifted the bridge. He removed the ebony tailpiece and saddle. Next, he carefully applied alcohol along the plate of the cello, where it was joined to the ribs. This he did several times.

He produced a thin knife and tried its blade edge on his thumb. Probing, he inserted it between the belly and the ribs of the cello. Mariana thought she might faint. He looked up, half smiling. "I have performed this operation hundreds of times, my dears, but never on so beautiful a patient."

They heard a scraping sound and then a series of squeaks, the wood complaining against the knife. Then they heard a shocking clap and a sundering groan as Fernand lifted the top free. He stood under the lamp's bright light. On the table lay the dismembered Swan.

As he walked Mariana home, Claude wrapped his arm around her. "I think you should contact the Met and speak with the Scotsman. If he makes a reasonable offer, it might be best to accept. The crack can be repaired, but it seems the word is out." She agreed.

⁂

On Claude's final morning in Manhattan, he played the Vuillaume in Mariana's living room. She lay on the couch, eyes closed. After running through his usual warm-up exercises, he turned to the Victor Herbert Cello Concerto No. 2 in E Minor, which he was preparing to play the next month in Munich. Mariana had performed it many times. It had been one of Feldmann's favorites. He'd praised the amplitude of its dramatic impact, the lilting melodic line in the Andante. Claude had listened often to Feldmann's recording of the concerto, with the Philadelphia

Orchestra, but he had never studied it with his mentor. Now he played for Mariana.

She listened intently. Lying back on the couch, languid, she opened her eyes and studied him. As he approached the end of the prologue, Mariana sat bolt upright, shouting, "Make the dog howl, Claude. You have to make the dog howl!"

He stared at her. "Excuse me?"

"It's what Alexander used to say. Our little spaniel would sit quietly all day in his studio when he was practicing or teaching. But she would go nuts when Alexander played the Victor Herbert. She would moan as if she played along with him during the slow movement, and howl during the Allegros. My father was delighted. He thought this was a sign of her great musical sensitivity. And whenever he felt I wasn't performing at the emotional level the music demanded—with any piece, not just the Herbert—he would shout at me, 'Make the dog howl!' It meant, 'Find the music; go deeper; give more. No other concerto ever made Maxxie howl, but Alexander would howl at me if he approved of something I'd done. It was his highest accolade. Now start again, Claude, from the very beginning."

First he laughed about the musical dog. Then, growing serious, he played again. She became his teacher, coaching him, singing along, stopping him to explain—with a ferocity similar to Alexander's but far less unkind—where Claude was failing the music. "You're playing the notes correctly, but you're not playing the music." How often she'd heard Feldmann say this, or, "Your playing teaches me nothing about life." And how many times she'd seen students in his master classes blanch and start to cry. "Oh, don't do that," she'd want to call out, "he hates tears. They make him mean. He'll think you don't have the inner strength to be an artist." But, of course, she didn't dare to interrupt, and when the student played again, the improvement was remarkable. Was that what it took? she had wondered. This could never be her way.

Claude went over and over the phrases until she told him to move on. For two hours, they proceeded in this fashion and when, at last, he performed the concerto again for her, from start to finish, she threw back her head and howled, "Arooooo!"

He smiled and thanked her. "That was a great help." Claude stood and handed Mariana the instrument. "Now, you play for me."

She started, again, to protest. He silenced her: "You promised."

"I didn't. There's nothing I'm prepared to play."

"I know that's true, because I've had your cello. Just play a single movement of a Bach suite. Anything. Play anything at all. I want to see you, to hear you play..."

Mariana took the chair. Claude settled himself on the couch, mopping his forehead and stretching his neck. She tuned again, plucking the strings and adjusting the bow. Then, brushing back her hair, she looked down in silence. She let that silence extend. Finally, lifting the bow to the strings, she began the Sarabande of Bach's Suite in D Minor. The haunting opening—slow, melancholy, contemplative—reflected what she was feeling. Her hands felt clumsy, her fingers weak; the double and triple stops were hard to maintain. Mariana knew that her technique, hampered by months of neglect, was less than perfect. And yet she played, reaching into the depths of the meditative, prayerful line, drawing out each phrase until she reached the final, whispered note.

She rested her head against the neck of the Vuillaume and closed her eyes. When she opened them, she saw that Claude was near tears. He had recognized the passionate restraint and sensitivity she shared with Alexander, their link direct. It was as if her father held the bow. Perhaps Claude could hear, as she could, what technique she'd lost since she'd stopped practicing four hours a day, years ago. But his expression told her that he understood what might have been and what remained of her great talent.

She put the cello down and sat next to him on the couch. Claude was ruminative. Suddenly, he threw back his head and howled, "Arooooo!"

Mariana giggled, swinging her legs over his. He stroked her hair, absently. Sipping coffee and looking at the Sunday *Times*, which Claude had brought with him, they spent the morning on the couch together. She leaned against him. In the filtered light, they talked about Alexander and Francine's love affair. "How they must have needed to plot and lie to be together," Mariana said. "I couldn't imagine a life of such stealth and deceit."

"For a while, perhaps," Claude answered, "but not for a lifetime. Did they not love each other enough?"

"It was Alexander," Mariana answered. "He never loved enough."

At noon, Claude looked at his watch, stretched, and stood. He took both her hands and drew her off the couch and into a long embrace, brushing his lips against her forehead. Although her heartbeat quickened, she opened the door to see him out.

CHAPTER EIGHTEEN

Mariana and Claude

2014

At seven o'clock on this October evening, guests cluster under the banners of the Bloomberg Court, exchanging greetings, drinking champagne, and lifting hors d'oeuvres off trays. Some inspect the display of medieval armor, the horses and swords and curiously small human figures swathed in metal and chain mail. Some study the halberds and pikes. One hundred of the museum's trustees and donors have been invited to a black-tie reception and lecture in the refurbished André Mertens Galleries for Musical Instruments. This evening's gala for supporters of the collection gives them an opportunity to see the great Silver Swan.

Chairs have been arranged at the center of the long, narrow display space around a carpeted platform that serves as a small stage. Three chairs have been placed there, one for Claude, one for Mariana, and one for Andrew Macintosh, the curator of musical instruments, who will introduce them.

"Fourteen years ago this very evening, ladies and gentlemen, I had the considerable pleasure of introducing the late, great Alexander Feldmann in this room. Some of you perhaps were present at that time also and remember the occasion:

we had the privilege of hearing Maestro Feldmann demonstrate and speak about his legendary instrument. That night Mr. Feldmann played his Stradivarius, the incomparable Silver Swan, and his daughter, Mariana, played a copy of it fashioned in the nineteenth century by Jean-Baptiste Vuillaume. Maestro Feldmann had made it his hobby, over many years, to commission reproductions of the cello by contemporary luthiers. There are now all together nine such copies.

"Tonight, Mariana Feldmann is here with us once more. Ms. Feldmann is a renowned cellist, teacher, and coach, invited all over the world to give master classes, teaching young cellists in the great tradition handed down by her father. Also with us tonight," Macintosh continues, "is the esteemed Swiss cellist Claude Roselle, a student of Feldmann's who has an international concert career and plays the Silver Swan on loan from our museum. He and Ms. Feldmann have made possible this great gift to the Mertens collection.

"Heretofore, the Batta-Piatigorsky Stradivarius of 1714 was the jewel of our collection. Now it's my honor to introduce you to a second great example of the master's craft—one built two years earlier by the great maker of Cremona, Anno Domini 1712. No other institution can lay claim to such a pair."

Claude and Mariana sit together on the small stage; the audience rises to applaud. In a gesture at least in part sentimental—though there is also an element of pride in her choice—she wears the floor-length silver gown she wore here with her father in 2000. It fits her still. Claude has a first touch of gray in his curls—but he is only thirty-nine and will retain his matinee-idol appearance for years. They make a striking pair.

"In truth, this great museum seeks to collect exactly what Alexander Feldmann sought in a long quest that ended in the dusty cabinet of a private house near Strasbourg: excellence in art. He wanted to find the instrument that best gave voice to his own sound, his musical ideas. For Piatigorsky, it was the Batta; for Bernard Greenhouse, the Countess of Stanlein; for Feldmann, the Silver Swan. Vowing to cherish and protect it forever, he hoped to ensure that this magnificent Stradivarius would be untarnished, its integrity unmarred. That will now be the responsibility of the Mertens Collection. Claude Roselle will keep its sound alive in concert halls—long may he do so!—and when he ceases to perform, the Swan will come back to this gracious room, for future admirers to see.

"You have come," Andrew Macintosh continues, "to hear these two fine artists play the greatest of instruments, not to listen to me. Now Ms. Feldmann and M. Roselle will play for you, together, the piece she and her father played when they were last here, the Sarabande of the Bach D-Minor Suite. M. Roselle will perform on the Vuillaume and Ms. Feldmann will play the Silver Swan."

Mariana stands and takes up the cello. The sheen of the wood retains the bright beauty that had cast its spell on her when young. There, on the right rear, is the faded patch where someone once spilled brandy and left a heart-shaped stain. Here, where Alexander rested his hand, there is an equivalent fading and, almost invisible because of Fernand's expert restoration, the sealed back crack.

She says, "My father dedicated his life to music. This splendid instrument was his friend, his constant companion for over forty-five years. He was a fortunate man to have had this honor. For him, the Stradivarius was only half itself when looked at and not heard; it was intended to be played. Hence, the museum, understanding this, has been generous in offering the Swan to Claude Roselle for the duration of his lifetime in music. This great cello, the Silver Swan, was my father's voice. Now it will sing for M. Roselle and, we both hope, for many generations to come."

As has been her lifelong habit, she touches the silver medallions fashioned by Cellini. After a long moment, Mariana raises her bow. She sits again. Her eyes meet Claude's, and they begin to play.

EPILOGUE

2018

Mariana is sitting by the pool in the garden at Swann's Way. The air is still and warm. She wears a faded sundress, from which her long legs extend over the end of the chaise longue. Her bare feet rub together to disturb a fly. It is mid-June and the effulgent peonies, which ran riot over her garden, have started to droop, the bees clustering to them as they flop over. She won't cut them back until fall; nothing about nature is unsightly, she believes. Nonetheless, the limp, dead flowers make her sad. The ground is carpeted with curled and fading petals, once so bright.

She hears the porch door open. A young woman wearing an apron approaches, notebook in hand. She crosses the garden to Mariana's chair.

"I have a few questions, Ms. Feldmann. I hate to disturb you."

"Don't be silly, Betty," Mariana says. She smiles up at her housekeeper. "I'm really just daydreaming."

"Do you have a final head count for the party tomorrow night? It's time to set the table."

"Final count, twenty. Unless Mr. Roselle's plane is delayed, then it's nineteen. But set a place for him, I'm fairly sure he'll get here in time."

"Fine. There won't be any weather problems, that's for sure. It's going to be a perfect summer day." She has written "twenty" in her notebook. "Also, I'm sorry to say your strawberries aren't quite ripe yet. Should we change our plan for dessert?"

"Whatever you think, Betty. You're in charge."

"It's hard to believe summer's here again, isn't it, Ms. Feldmann? Seems like you give this party every other month, not just once a year."

Mariana opens the Tanglewood season every year with a grand dinner. Although she tries to coordinate with Claude's arrival, it's not always possible. She enjoys the yearly return and sojourn of her half brother. He comes for two and a half months to participate in the Tanglewood Festival, to play at Ravinia in Chicago, Mostly Mozart in New York, at Caramoor, and in other summer concert series.

Despite Francine's disapproval, Claude and Mariana remain friends; they are comfortable with each other. Francine made only one attempt to communicate with Mariana, in 2011, sending her a note that said, "I always, for all those years, tried to do what was best for your family." Mariana did not answer. She and Francine do not speak, and Claude no longer allows Francine to mention his half sister's name; in her old age, she must accept things as they are.

Mariana makes her home at Swann's Way. A year after her father's death, she began to teach. Her reputation has grown and she is now in great demand, training the next generation of cellists. During the year, she travels to give master classes in America and Europe, but she is always grateful to return home. She has made Swann's Way her own and treasures the mountains' silence, which she hears as music.

Summers with Claude in residence are full and pleasurable. Once he arrives, after a year of concertizing, they have their routines. The Swan resumes its place on the Steinway's paisley cloth. During the week they walk together and practice their instruments, then share lunch on the back porch—fully restored since the fire. In the afternoons, they go to work, Claude to rehearse and Mariana to meet her classes at Tanglewood. In the community, the nature of their relationship is a matter of interest and speculation.

This summer, for the first time, Claude's son, Martin, will come for two weeks. Age seven, Martin studies the cello, and he has—his father says with pride—a special talent. Mariana looks forward to getting to know the boy and hearing him play.

Although it causes Claude some discomfort, he is pleasant, if not cordial, to her suitor, Nathan Epstein, a professor of French literature at Harvard. Engaged in writing an extensive and, he hopes, definitive literary biography of Proust, Nathan's curiosity had been aroused when he noticed the sign for Swann's Way while driving along the back roads of Stockbridge. Who would name a home after Proust's great novel? He turned up the driveway and knocked on the imposing front door. Mariana appeared. She told him of the Silver Swan and explained that her father had never read Proust, but he liked the conflation of the Swan, his famous cello, and Proust's *Un amour de Swann*. They shared a laugh. She invited him in for coffee. That was two years ago.

Nathan spends long weekends with Mariana, returning to Cambridge during the week to teach and write. When Claude arrives, he and Nathan speak to each other only in French. Mariana finds this frustrating; her own fluency is limited. But she accepts it as the nature of the friendship between these two men.

Now Mariana lies on her chaise, eyes closed against the brilliant sun, musing about Alexander. After all, she thinks, he had not deserted her or her mother. She had heard him describe himself publicly as a devoted father and husband. But so often when he spoke of himself, he sounded to Mariana as if he were describing someone else. How well did Alexander understand himself? she wonders. She thinks the answer is that he didn't know himself at all, not because he was incapable but because he simply had no interest in or gift for introspection. He studied only what he cared about—music, the making of music.

And what had he given her? she asks herself. If not attention, if not his interest in her life or a notion of happiness beyond the fulfillment of her talent as a cellist, if not the Silver Swan itself, what had he given her?

Slowly sitting up, she finds the answer. Alexander gave her music. Not the music she performed on stage, not the career, not the search for fame, but exquisite music itself—the capacity to hear it, feel it, play it, and be transported by it to a place of beauty and solace. "These gifts from Alexander," she tells herself, "are not nothing."

Swinging her legs off the chaise, she goes to the house to make place cards for the dinner. Before entering the kitchen, she sits on a porch rocker and brushes the grass off her feet.

❦

The whole hillside is ablaze. Strands of small white lights line the driveway and twist around the branches of the trees and the bushes surrounding the house. Mariana has turned on lamps in every room and thrown open the double front doors. The chandelier illumines the foyer and the grand winding staircase. It is eight o'clock. The sky has turned a dusky purple, though to the west the mountaintops are still rimmed in rose.

Wineglass in hand, she stands at the doorway, enjoying the evening air before her guests arrive. At forty-six, Mariana Alexandra Feldmann believes one must *learn* to be happy. Like music, it takes discipline, commitment, and desire. Her work has been fruitful. Peering into the growing dark, she sees the headlights of the first car winding up the side of the mountain. It churns the driveway's gravel and comes to a stop. Behind it, a parade of cars slowly climbs toward her, lights flickering through the trees. She descends the front steps to welcome her friends.

ACKNOWLEDGMENTS

To my beloved, late mentor, Mary Delia Flory, who, in the autumn of 1960, presented me with a journal of blank pages in which she had written, "For your first novel," I express my deepest gratitude. Huge thanks as well to Alison Hine, my teacher and guide of many decades, for her encouragement. And in remembrance of my parents, Bernard and Aurora Greenhouse, who surrounded me with music and whom I miss every day.

I offer my heartfelt gratitude to dear friends, John and Nina Darnton, who introduced me to my agent, the inimitable Kathy Robbins, who introduced me to the remarkable publisher of Other Press, Judith Gurewich, who introduced me both to this new adventure in publication and to her wonderful husband, Victor.

For her thoughtful and sensitive readings of *The Silver Swan*, I am indebted to Kathryn Frank, editor and dear friend extraordinaire. And to the many lovely people at The Robbins Office and Other Press—Yvonne E. Cárdenas, Marjorie DeWitt, Katherine DiLeo, Micah Hauser, and Anjali Singh—I am grateful for your time and help. To my family of writers: Francesca (fiction), Andrea (journalism), Nicholas Stoller (movies), and Alexander Shalom (legal treatises); and to my granddaughters, Anna, Penelope, Rosalie, and Frederica, thank you for giving meaning to all the hours of my life.

And to Nicholas Delbanco, my husband of forty-four years and friend for ten before . . . oh, where to begin? With love from start to finish.